GW01606873

Other Books by Liz Rain

Perks of Office

ONSIDE Play

LIZ RAIN

Acknowledgements

Thank you to Astrid Ohletz and Ylva Publishing for all the work you have put into *Onside Play* and for putting it out into the world.

Thanks to content editor Miranda Miller and copy editor Sheena Billett for doing an excellent job and putting up with so much Aussie slang and soccer lingo.

A huge thanks also to my sensitivity reader Tori Aundrea Moore for your thoughtful and considered feedback. The sapphic fiction community is very lucky to have you as part of it!

A big shout out to the ever-supportive Lee Winter for your assist on the goal line in the last seconds of extra time.

I would also like to acknowledge the traditional owners of the land on which this book was written—the Turrbul and Jaggera peoples of the Yugambeh region. I pay my respects to their elders past, present, and emerging. The story of Australia's First Nations' people is one of strength and resilience, and I thank them for their continuing custodianship of land, water, and culture.

Dedication

For Dani. The best thing I got out of soccer was you.

Chapter 1

Melbourne, Australia
2023

In the grey half-light, I fumbled around on the floor for my clothes. Undies! Yes! Slung over the back of an armchair. I pulled them on and turned a full circle, looking for the remainder of my outfit.

Geez! This was the biggest hotel room I'd ever been in.

I tapped my phone screen, hoping the extra illumination might help me in my search. 6:15 a.m. A normal wake-up time for me but probably not for—

"Keeley?" A thick, muffled voice drifted from across the room.

I sat on the edge of the bed. The woman lying there rolled onto her back and swept the blonde hair out of her eyes. She cleared her throat and grimaced.

I handed her a plastic bottle of water from the bedside table, and she sat up and took one big swig, then another few gulps. She had the bedsheet swathed around her hips and was wearing a Kylie Minogue T-shirt.

I smiled. Amber Hatfield was an internationally famous pop singer, but right now she didn't look much like her magazine shoots or album covers.

I was into this bleary, tousled look though. "A bit dusty, hey?"

She squinted and nodded. "Totally. Whoever in my crew got that top-shelf bottle of bourbon half an hour before the bar closed is on my shit list." She leaned back against the neutral-toned headboard and raised an eyebrow. "Good night, though."

It wasn't a question. It was a summation. A kick of attraction made me blink. I'd had my share of one-night stands, especially the last couple of years since I'd been playing soccer at the highest level in Australia. Some were underwhelming, some were downright call-in-the-national-guard disasters, but some were awesome. This one had definitely been in the awesome category.

I enjoyed listening to her mixed-up accent. She'd been living over in the States for five years, trying to turn Australian pop music success into an international career. She'd told me she quite liked the hustle required to get a foot on the bottom rung of the American industry. Being a household name here at home was nice though, and being able to do a sold-out Aussie tour to pay the bills every now and then was very handy.

She hadn't flinched at all when she'd said she was a household name. She had an unashamed grit to her—a confidence. It was sexy as hell.

"A very good night," I said.

"But you're heading off?"

"Yep. I've got training in less than two hours."

She crinkled her nose. "Aw. You're sure I can't convince you to stay?"

She brushed her lips against my jawline.

I gave a full-body shiver. "I'm a weak woman. Do *not* tempt me." I put my hand to the side of her face and kissed her lips gently. "But I do have to go. Can I turn this light on? I can't for the life of me find my clothes."

She grinned and switched on the lamp. I jumped up and kept on with my quest. My shirt was under the coffee table.

She propped up a couple of pillows and lay down again with a sigh. "I'd help, but I'm enjoying the spectacle."

I picked up a cushion to throw at her. "Ooh, my jeans are under here."

My throw landed way wide and bounced off the edge of the bed and onto the floor.

She shook her head. "Poor effort, McGee. Lucky you chose soccer and not netball. You'd never make the national team with that arm."

I laughed as I pulled my jeans up. "You're funny, you know. If this, uh, singing business doesn't work out for you, you could always try stand-up."

All right. Shoes on? Check. Phone in pocket? Running hideously late? Double check.

I sat back down next to her. She rolled onto her side toward me.

We did an identical tight-lipped half-smile.

"This bit is always awkward," she said. "My one-night stands are never sure how to get the tone of their farewells right."

I noted the use of the term "one-night stand." It wasn't the first time she'd used it since we'd met. She had also explicitly spelt out to me the night before that she was only after a casual hook-up.

I preferred to keep things simple too, so I was happy to go along with her terms. "Never? How many have you had?"

"Oh, hundreds. Same as you."

"Hah! Well, I *never* get the tone of anything I say right, so I just tell the truth." I took a big, loud breath in and opened my eyes very wide. And I did want to do right by her. The launch event the night before held by the TV station airing the Women's World Cup had been boring until I had started chatting with Amber, who had recorded the official song for the tournament.

Amber smiled. "Yikes, I'm bracing myself."

I exhaled, and my words came out in a rush. "You're nice and funny and smart and good at sex, and I had a really good time. I'm glad I wandered over to your crazy entourage at the bar last night to see what the hell was going on." I leaned over uncomfortably and lay my head on the pillow next to hers. "You've got my number, and I hope you'll text me when you're in Melbourne next. Or Brisbane or Stockholm because I live in those places sometimes too."

"Weird flex mentioning all your residences, but thanks. I'm glad you bumbled over too. You're really good at flirting and equally good at everything that came after too." She kissed my mouth, lingering just a little and taking a hold of the sleeve of my shirt. Then she rested her head back on the pillow.

I stood. "See you around?"

"You betcha."

I turned back at the door and held up my hand as a good-bye.

She stretched her long legs out. "Hit me up if you're ever in LA, Nashville, or Sydney. See, other people can have three houses too."

I grinned and shook my head as I walked down the silent hallway toward the lifts. My blurred reflection in the burnished metal of the lift doors showed I was pretty dishevelled. I thanked all the lesbian deities that my night-on-the-town look was jeans, expensive sneakers, and a T-shirt. I was on a pretty classic walk of shame right now, but it wasn't as obvious as if I had been wearing a little black dress, stilettos, and inch-thick make-up.

I yawned, then grimaced. At twenty-five I was getting way too old for this. I needed to take everyone's advice and cut out the late nights before training. It was against team rules to drink while the season was in full swing, so I never did. But that didn't ever stop a late dinner with mates turning into barhopping and dancing. And if an attractive girl ever made eyes at me, well, I was only human after all.

I walked quickly through the lobby but stopped short. A group of a few dozen people hung around the entryway. Was it some kind of protest? Maybe the hotel was owned by a conglomerate that dumped toxic waste on seals, then clubbed them for good measure.

A few of them had signs. The closest was a piece of pink cardboard with a picture of Amber's face with a big glitter love heart around it.

Uh-oh. I considered heading out into the throng, not making eye contact, and hurrying through and away. It seemed like it could be easy, but my brain was a bit fuzzy from tiredness, and it was hard to think.

Just then, behind the gathered crowd, a bus rolled by with my picture on it, my big white face smiling, my big body wearing the distinctive green-and-gold jersey of the Australian Matildas national soccer team, an electricity company's logo floating in thin air to the left of my artfully ruffled short hairdo. I closed my eyes and lowered my head. *Think, Keeley.*

It was likely someone in this crowd would recognise me. I'd been playing for one of the Melbourne soccer teams for three years now and for the Australian team for two. Interest in women's soccer was reaching an all-time high in the lead-up to the World Cup, which was starting in a few weeks. It used to be that I would get recognised at about a third of the places I went, but the advertising blitz for the World Cup—I was on the telly, spruiking everything from major supermarket chains to obscure protein powders—meant it was happening more and more.

If I was seen leaving the hotel Amber Hatfield was staying at in the early morning—that wasn't weird, right? I could have any number of reasons to be there.

But a memory surfaced of a little clutch of people gathered outside the bar as we were trying to leave the night before. Amber had told me there were a few fans who studied her entourage's social media stories and tried to piece together where she was. Or sometimes some rando would snap a photo and put it on social media, and if they tagged her or used the right hashtag, the fans would find her.

"Wow, um, what do you think about all that?" I'd asked her. It sounded like a living nightmare to me, and that might have come across in my voice.

She shrugged. "Par for the course, I guess. I've been at this since I was seventeen, so a few of them are pretty rusted on."

Security had moved that crowd on before we went outside, but if any of them were still hanging around, they would have seen me with her the night before.

Shit. I didn't know if it would be a big deal for her if these people knew we'd hooked up. She had kind of a clean-cut image. Super clean, in fact—one of her big hits of about five years ago had just been used for a laundry detergent TV ad.

Back toward the lifts, a woman in a dark polo pushed a cleaner's trolley.

I half-jogged over to her. "Hi. Um, is there another way out of here? I'm, er, in a hurry and want to avoid that crowd out there."

She shrugged. "Yeah, there's another way. Come on." She pressed the lift button. "Hey, I know you. You play tennis?"

I glanced over my shoulder at the front desk. The well-groomed man behind it was staring at his computer screen. "Soccer."

"Oh, yeah, yeah, yeah. You're on the supermarket ad. You kick the orange, and the cricket lady catches it. I love that ad! Hey, can I get a selfie?"

"Sure thing." She pulled out her phone, and we took the pic.

The lift dinged, and the doors opened. I went in, and she followed but left her trolley outside. She swiped a card on a stretchy string attached to her belt and hit the button for car park 1.

"Look for the big car gates. There's a door next to it, then some steps up to street level. If you turn the handle, the door will open. There's big red letters saying an alarm will sound and you should use it only in an emergency, but it's not true. You'll be right."

The lift door threatened to close on her.

"Oh my God, thank you so much. You're a legend," I said.

She stepped back from the door and grabbed hold of her trolley. The doors started closing.

"Yeah, no worries at all. And good luck at the World Cup."

When the lift dinged open again, I walked out into the grey undercover carpark.

"Oof," I said as the cold hit me.

I picked up my pace and followed the big arrows that pointed toward the exit. The door was right where my new mate had said it would be, and I pushed through it and jogged up the concrete steps. When I neared the top, I pulled out my phone to check the time again. *Bugger!* There was no way I wasn't going to be late.

"Oi, watch it!" said a male voice.

I'd walked into the back of someone wearing a big puffy jacket. "Sorry!"

Uh-oh. Puffer-jacket guy was one of a crowd of about ten people. Ten people wearing Amber Hatfield tour T-shirts and hoodies. They all turned to look at me. One held a framed A3 poster of Amber, and one teenage girl even had a full-size cardboard cut-out of her. A woman held two CD cases in each hand and a permanent marker in her mouth.

I had no filter at the best of times, but it did an even worse job when I was surprised or stressed. "Aren't you meant to be out the front?" *And who still has CDs? How long have you had these albums?*

Puffer-jacket guy narrowed his eyes. "A few of us always set up near the back gate in case she leaves by car."

I got a little chill down the back of my neck at the way he said *always*, followed by a flash of annoyance at my new mate on the hotel cleaning crew. Surely she hadn't set me up to walk into this small but passionate mob at the back entrance? I dismissed the idea—she had liked my dumb grocery ad! And that one had been particularly irritating.

"Hey," said CD woman. "Don't you play cricket or something?"

I tensed. "Errrrrr…"

"Yeah," puffer-jacket guy said. "I know you. You're on that ad for milk where the cow's wearing a tutu."

My heart pounded. He was right.

A few people nodded, including cardboard cut-out girl. "Gimme a second. It'll come to me. Kasey MacWhirter!"

My pits began to sweat despite the early morning cold.

"No, that's not it," said CD woman. "Katie something?"

"Kylie! Kylie? Nope, that's not it."

I turned tail and ran down the narrow, cobbled alleyway Melbourne had so many of.

"Hey, where's she going?" someone yelled.

Footsteps pounded behind me. I swore under my breath. The mob was probably bored out of their brains waiting around for a possible sighting of Amber. A chase was the most exciting thing that could happen—second only to getting a wave from Amber through a tinted car window.

I made a right into an even smaller alleyway. "Ah, bollocks!" It was a dead end, with a big dumpster in front of an old brick wall.

The footsteps behind me grew louder.

I ran forward and stumbled on the old cobblestones. "Shit! Stupid bloody Melbourne and its stupid bloody old-timey alleyways. Get real streets, why dontcha."

I righted myself and took a flying leap onto the closed lid of the bin.

"What the hell?" said a winded voice behind me.

It sounded like puffer-jacket guy, but I didn't look around to check. I hauled myself up and sat on top of the wall. The other side was a sheer drop. I closed my eyes, trying not to think about how mad the team physios would be if I broke both my ankles, and jumped. I landed in a crouch on the cement. I took a deep breath and gave myself a check over for any major injury. I was ok! I jumped up and looked skyward. Adrenaline still pumped around my body as well as a surge of elation. Escape! It was primal, like I was a cavewoman who'd outrun a sabre-tooth tiger.

I took off at a jog toward Lonsdale Street. I put a bit of distance between me and Amber's crazy fans before calling an Uber to take me home for the quickest costume change ever. And she wouldn't even have to know the lengths I'd gone to in an attempt to protect her privacy.

I smiled to myself. Success!

Chapter 2

I WAS TEN MINUTES LATE to training, but otherwise the session had gone off without a hitch. Back at home, my head full of cotton-wool after a long nap, I reached for my phone to check the time. I almost dropped it again. My lock screen was chock full of message notifications.

I sat up and fumbled, swiping to reveal them all. My adrenaline surged. Was Melbourne in some kind of emergency situation, and I had been snoozing so soundly I'd missed the whole thing?

Hahahaha! Bin' good knowing ya, mate! Coach is going to spit-roast you.

Bewildered, I scrolled through to the earliest text, where one of my teammates had sent me a link to a gossip website.

It turned out that the photos of me leaping over the industrial bin that morning had been put alongside photos of me and Amber at dinner the night before, and the story was doing the rounds of the internet. I scrolled through a few more texts roasting the hell out of me, then held my head in my hands.

I had to be an idiot to get everything so wrong. I should have gone home straight after dinner, or gotten Amber's number and phoned her many months from now when the World Cup was a distant memory. Or at least I should have left after we had sex, under the cover of darkness before her mob arrived. Or this morning I should have said to her fans, “No, I’m nobody at all! I must just have one of those faces!” and walked off nonchalantly, instead of sprinting off like a criminal who’d been rumbled by the cops.

I shut my eyes as another stab of anxiety got me in the gut. *Amber.* I’d gotten her all mixed up in this mess too. I scrabbled in my bedsheets to retrieve my phone, found her newly-entered contact details and hit the call button.

“Well hello there,” she said.

“Hi.”

“I hear you’ve taken up parkour. Or were you just so deathly ashamed of having spent the night with me that you would do anything to evade capture?”

“Oh geez, I am *so* sorry. I know how this must look—”

She laughed. “Dude, chill. I’m kidding around.”

I took a deep breath. My churn of worry and regret eased.

“I’m dying to know why you ran off from Darren, the esteemed Mr President of my fan club. Did he start on his rant about how it’s a national disgrace I’ve never been nominated for a Grammy?”

“Darren? Does he wear a puffy jacket?”

“Almost exclusively.”

Now I knew she wasn’t mad I started to enjoy the archness in her voice. She had a great voice—rich and melodious. I guess it *was* her full-time job after all.

“Well, I, uh… Your fans were all there this morning and I kind of freaked out. I didn’t know if they should know you brought strange people back to your hotel, especially strange, you know, women. Your fan club has kind of a wholesome, white picket fence vibe.”

I had to pull the phone away from my ear as she shouted with laughter. Then snorted. Then laughed some more.

“Aw bless your little heart. It’s so refreshing that you obviously have not followed my career, not for one second. The title track of my second album is called ‘Use My Body.’ The video was banned in eighteen countries. And I was engaged to a DJ named Alyssa Vixen for ten months in 2017.”

“Oh. I’ve heard of her. She’s played Coachella.” I sighed and looked at the ceiling. “I really am a moron.”

"Hey, no. You're a bit of a dope, but it's sweet you were trying to protect my honour. Totally unnecessary, but sweet. Hey, my publicity team is getting all kinds of calls. Do you need them to refute any of the story or are you happy to roll with it?"

"I haven't even read the whole story."

She gasped. "Oh, but you must! It's sooooo funny. I mean, sorry… but it really is. Read it now."

"All right, I'll put you on speaker."

"Google *dumpster jumper* and it should come up."

I groaned. The first search result was a headline on the trashy website of the English *Daily Herald.*

Dumpster jumper at dawn—Steamy hotel tryst with sexy singer ends in soccer star's bizarre escape.

The "story" consisted of blurry photos of me and Amber, taken through the window of the restaurant the night before, one of us leaving together, then about six action shots of me jumping up onto the bin and scaling the wall.

I slumped back down onto my bed. "I look so bloody sketchy. My eyes are bloodshot! Did they doctor the photos?"

"Look, probably. But, hey now, I think you look cute. Your arse looks great in that one captioned: *Keeley McGee fleeing the alley.* Do you think they meant it to rhyme?"

I chuckled. If Amber could see the funny side, at least that was something. "Thanks. At least my arse isn't hanging out. Thank heavens I resisted when they tried to bring back low-rise jeans."

"Do you need my people to deny it was a tryst? Say we spent the night playing backgammon and eating crumpets?"

"Crumpets? Is that what the kids are calling it these days?"

"Hah! I'm serious though. Are you in trouble with the team?"

I grimaced. "I think I'll get a stern talking-to, but I didn't breach any team rules. I'm not doing any more dumb shit until *after* the World Cup, though. The worst thing we can do is get caught out in a lie. Because, if I remember rightly, we didn't play backgammon and put the kettle on. We…"

"We banged."

"We totally banged."

She laughed again. "My manager's thrilled. No such thing as bad publicity in his book. He thinks we might get a bump in ticket sales for the rest of the tour."

I smiled. "I'm glad to hear it. Apparently everyone on lesbian twitter reckons I like to play the field a bit. That fact has never made it into the mainstream media before, but no harm done as far as I'm concerned."

"'Play the field'—I like what you did there."

"Oh yeah. Puns are how I reel all the girls in."

She scoffed. "Hey, I've gotta go. They're calling me for sound check. It takes ages to get the levels right in an arena."

"Is that meant to impress me? Because it does."

"You don't fool me. Millions of people are going to watch you play in the World Cup. I'll be there cheering you on."

"Starting up a 'dumpster jumper' chant in the crowd, I bet."

"Hah! Something like that. Does the *Daily Herald* not know they're called skip bins in this country? They missed a trick with 'skip skipper.'"

"Just another sign real journalism is down the toilet. Hey, I'll let you get to your sound check."

"Okay, see ya. Make sure you call me again, if you've got the time to hang out for a night while jetsetting between your three residences."

"I'll make the time. Sure thing. Bye."

The one shining light in this shit storm was the discovery that Amber Hatfield was a class act. I was attracted to her, but it was like she drew me in by being funny and sexy and cool on the one hand, and at the same time insisted on keeping me at arm's length. Being with her on more than a "casual hook-up" basis would probably mean an epic case of emotional whiplash.

To many of my serial monogamist friends, a first date as good as last night's would have put them automatically into girlfriend mode. I'd seen it again and again—the robot voice sounding the alarm in their heads: *'Lock it down. Lock it down.'* That game wasn't for me, though. When I cared and tried, it ended in heartbreak.

A name came unbidden into my head. *Christine.* I tapped into Instagram and started to type the name in. I only needed to type the first two letters. It was my guilty little secret how often I looked up my ex on socials, but my search history knew exactly why I was there.

The first photo was one I hadn't seen before. I sighed. Christine Delacourt, a stunning black woman, smiled into the camera as her girlfriend Cora Helgesen, a stunning white woman, planted a kiss on her cheek. They were dressed casually with the ocean in the background. I went into the kitchen and started to fill up the biggest glass we had with water.

The little trip down memory lane had lowered my spirits even further. I shook my head. Wasn't the definition of insanity doing the same thing over and over again and expecting a different result? But I had been checking in on Christine's posts more often as the days counted down until I would see her again.

Christine and I had dated when we were both on the Florida State University soccer team years before. She had made a meteoric rise from college soccer to the US National Team in record time.

Australia would play the US in our first match of the upcoming World Cup. And it would be the first time I'd had any contact with Christine since we broke up.

I stared out the window at the tiny patch of lawn at the back of the old two-storey terrace I shared with a couple of housemates in the Melbourne suburb of Footscray. I shook my head. It was actually nuts that I was thinking about Christine right now instead of the fact I was probably in big trouble with the leadership team at the Matildas. I would put her out of my mind completely, and work on a plan to get back in the good books.

"Christine freaking Delacourt," said a voice behind me.

I whirled, spilling water from my overfilled glass.

Viv, my former college roommate and current Footscray housemate stood brandishing my phone, which I had left unlocked on the bench. She had gotten a Bachelor of Fine Arts in musical theatre in college and I had done marketing on a full international soccer scholarship. We were like chalk and cheese in a lot of ways but we had been tight back in college and over the years she had become my best friend in the whole world. She was tiny and fair like a modern-day Tinkerbell, but my adrenaline spiked at the sight of her.

"Oi, give that back or I'll called the privacy police. You've breached all my rights!" I said.

"Sprung, sprung, sprung. Creeping on the ex. How many times have we talked about this, Keels?"

"Me creeping? You're the one spying on my defenceless and unsuspecting phone!"

She held up her hand like she was reciting the Pledge of Allegiance. She was from North Carolina so definitely knew it. "I take no responsibility. You know I'm drawn to shiny, colourful things."

I slumped.

Viv shook her head and put her hands on my shoulders. "Look, you know I've never gotten to play a villain in any of my productions because—"

"Because you're too sweet-looking. Yes, I know." I scowled, knowing exactly where this was going.

"But I know a thing or two about them. Now, I am not going to stand here and say that Christine Delacourt is evil to the core." She lifted her eyebrows and leaned toward me, telegraphing to the audience in the very back row that there was a very good chance Christine was, in fact, evil to the core. "It's like that line from *Forrest Gump*."

"Life is like a box of chocolates?"

"No, Keeley," she rolled her eyes. "Stupid is as stupid does," she said in a cadence that was straight from Alabama.

My mouth dropped open. "Whoa, whoa, whoa! I may be a little weak but I'm not stupid."

"No, look, stop interrupting and let me get to my point. Forrest's mom makes the point that nobody *is* anything. It's how they act that you judge them on. Christine treated you in a thoughtless and mean way, and I for one am not in a hurry to forget it.

"When someone shows you who they are, you best believe them. I sometimes think she showed you her true self right from the beginning and you've been making excuses to yourself about her ever since."

She pressed her lips together and patted my shoulder.

I was happy the pity party was interrupted by the return of our other housemate Fletch. They loped into the room and grinned. Lanky, non-binary, and easily the most easygoing person I had in my life, they were a welcome sight, as usual. They'd joined the Matildas the same year as me, and we'd hit it off right away. When they were traded from Adelaide United to Melbourne Victory the year before, I'd invited them to move in with me and Viv.

"What are we talking about?" Fletch asked.

"Christine Delacourt," said Viv.

"Oh yeah?" They opened up the fridge and stuck their head in.

I scowled at Viv.

She poked her tongue out at me.

"You've never played against her, have you Mac?" asked Fletch, perching on a bar stool at the counter.

"Nope. I went over to the Olympics with the team but didn't play the game against the US. And she had a calf strain or something and didn't play in those two friendly matches in Portland a couple of years ago."

"She's a deadset gun, mate. She tore us up at the Olympics. You'll have the main job on her at the Cup if you're at right-back."

"Keeley can take her. They played together at Florida State."

"Really? I didn't know that," said Fletch.

"Just for one semester. We didn't know each other well. Anyway." I scanned the room and caught sight of a pile of dishes on the bench. "It's my turn to clean the kitchen. I'd better, you know, make a start. On that."

"Yeah, mate. We'll leave you to it," said Fletch. "Hey, does your new-found interest in waste disposal mean you want to take the bins out too?"

"Oh, ha, ha, ha," I said at Fletch's and Viv's retreating backs.

I reached to switch my phone off, glancing quickly at the photo on the screen.

Had Christine shown me her true self right from the beginning? When I thought back to that senior year of college, the actual events got all muddled up and overpowered by the intense emotions of that time.

Chapter 3

2019

I HAD FIRST MET CHRISTINE a few weeks into my final year at Florida State. I had been running late for training. Being roommates with Viv meant I was dragged to many a community theatre production, and that day's matinee performance of *Sweeney Todd* had run late.

When I arrived Coach already had the team grouped in the centre of the pitch.

I had thrown my bag down and run toward them, slowing to an ungainly hop to fasten my left shinguard. Coach's authoritative voice carried through the still air as I reached the group.

"…and *this* is Keeley McGee," she said.

Every eye turned toward me. For a moment the only sound was the cicadas starting up for the evening.

"Keeley, I was just taking our new recruit through our team expectations. Would you be so kind as to fill her in please?"

My insides withered. Although Coach looked cool as a cucumber, I had thrown off the rhythm of her opening address to the newbie, and she wasn't happy about it.

"Um, Responsibility, Accountability and Excellence," I said.

"That's right! Now, FSU was lucky enough to get our new team member on a full scholarship, and I was kind and generous enough to loan her to team US to compete in the recent under-23's World Cup in Reykjavik, which they won without dropping a single game. But now she's back, she's here, and she's ready to help us win the pennant this year. Christine Delacourt!" Coach started clapping, and everyone joined in.

Christine appeared unfazed by this WWE-level introduction. She looked about my age, tall, and insanely fit-looking. She could have just stepped out of a Nike catalogue. Her hair was pulled back into a short ponytail, and her headband matched her shoelaces. She was all class, and I suddenly felt even more red-faced and flustered by comparison.

"Thanks, Coach. I'm glad to be here." Her voice was clear and resonant.

"Now, because Keeley did not demonstrate enough 'Responsibility' in terms of being here on time," Coach said, "instead of the exciting drills I had planned, you are all going to run laps."

There was a muted chorus of groans.

I wasn't even a lap and a half around before I was drenched in sweat. You would think being from Logan, Queensland, Australia—a city wedged between the sub-tropical city of Brisbane and the beaches of the Gold Coast—that I was built for heat and humidity. However, my sandy complexion, pre-disposition to red-facedness and sweatiness were irrefutable proof that my ancestors had made a grave error when they emigrated from Scotland. My uncle's *ancestry.com* research had revealed a number of them had died of "exposure" while trying to establish farms in the outback.

This was my fourth and final year at Florida State University and I was just shy of my twenty-second birthday. I had showed enough in the under-18 comps back home, and been able to come to FSU on a coveted full scholarship for soccer.

I had managed to start the school year off on a good note, but now it looked like now I had taken a giant step backwards.

When the training session was over and we were walking back to the dorms, I fell into step with the new girl, Christine. She had managed to run more laps than anyone in the time Coach had given us.

"Hi," I began.

She didn't answer but turned her head to look at me.

"I'm Keeley."

"Yes, I remember Coach introducing you when you arrived." She didn't say it, but the "…late" hung in the air.

"Uhhh, yeah. So, you're on a scholarship?" She didn't reply so I continued. "Me too. Full international scholarship. I'm studying marketing. How about you?"

"Sports science."

"Oh, cool. Those guys always throw the best parties. They're all so fit and strong though, it's hard to keep up on the dance floor. Hey, let me know if you want me to introduce you around." The group had stopped at one of the quads, about to disperse.

"Thanks, but I'm not here to go to parties. Just because my tuition's free doesn't mean I'm not going to take it seriously. And I take my soccer equally as seriously." And with that she walked off, not waiting for anyone who might happen to be walking the same way.

A few weeks later I dropped my gym bag on the floor of the University of Virginia "Away" change room in Charlottesville. A freshman named Renee dropped hers too and sat down on the bench. She rubbed her hands up and down the tops of her thighs.

I smiled at her. "Nervous?"

She nodded and her face turned from pale to a slight tinge of green.

I sat down next to her and put my arm on her shoulder. "Hey, it's going to be all right."

Her eyebrows creased. "I just wish Coach wouldn't keep going on about how we have to win this comp to make the NCAA this year. It's been my dream since I was five to win that comp, and today's the day I can start to make it happen." She breathed out and gave a little shudder. "Or fuck it up entirely."

"Can I give you some advice?"

She rested her elbows on her knees and held her head, but gave a small nod.

"Don't try to fight your nerves. Feel them, acknowledge them—but don't worry about them. Just go through your prep and warm-up and listen to Coach. The extra adrenaline will supercharge your speed and endurance if you harness it and use it."

She lifted her head and pressed her lips together in a tight smile, looking a shade more normal. "Thanks, I'll try."

The physio called her over and she jumped up.

"The inexperienced ones don't need more power, they need more control."

I hadn't noticed Christine unpacking her bag next to me. I sighed, not caring if she heard me. "Is that so?"

She glanced sideways at me and shrugged. "I just thought if you're going to go around offering free sports psychology it might as well be right."

My face burned. I stood up. "What is your problem? I was just trying to make her feel better."

She stopped rummaging and looked square at me. "In my experience, teams operate better if everyone focusses on their own performance and doesn't mess with one another's feelings."

"Well, that must be very easy for you because you don't have any!"

I picked up my bag and huffed to the other side of the changeroom, putting it down next to our team captain, Naomi, a bit harder and more noisily than I'd meant to.

"Jeez, Keeley. Save that aggro for the opposition."

"I'm sorry, I know. It's just that Christine is, like, the literal worst. Bloody hell. It's like she's a robotic prototype developed secretly to win soccer matches. But they messed up and didn't give her any feelings, so no one will believe she's human."

Naomi raised an eyebrow and shook her head.

"What? The whole plan will fall over because nobody will be fooled."

She scoffed then took me by the shoulders. "You sound nuts. Can you get your head in the game please, before your nonsense starts to distract everyone?"

I dropped my head a little. "Yes, skipper."

"Look, Blake gets along with her just fine." She gestured to the two of them, smiling and chatting while they used big, hot-pink bands to stretch their shoulders. “We all get on with her just fine. You’re a senior player, so it’s up to you to help her fit in.”

The stands were filling up with people decked out in Virginia’s navy blue and orange. A watery autumn afternoon sunshine tried to break through the misty mountain clouds but couldn’t quite manage it. I was glad, because a defender’s bane is afternoon sun in the eyes which can lead to an error that, from the shady stands or coach’s box, might look completely unforced. I started my last stretches and noticed Christine shielding her eyes and looking up toward the pale sun.

She had her arm outstretched and her hand upright, fingers splayed like she was checking her manicure. I narrowed my eyes then scoffed when I realised she was estimating how long it would take the sun to dip below the roof of the western stand.

“Hey Claire. Check out Copernicus over there.” I cocked my head toward Christine.

Christine inhaled sharply and dropped her hand. Claire, our best midfielder, rolled her eyes and shook her head at me before turning away to do some deep lunges.

“The wind’s picked up,” Christine said to nobody in particular. “Defence better hope the sun drops before those clouds clear. They’ll be looking right into it in the first half.”

I scowled and looked straight up. “Forwards better…um…make sure they don’t get too distracted by chatting about the weather with all their friends and forget where the goals are.” *Ok, so not my best zinger ever, but she’s being ridiculous!*

Christine narrowed her eyes, then ran off in the opposite direction and grabbed a ball from the net bag.

Back in the change rooms I whipped my jersey off and flung it onto the floor. My throat was tight and I sat, hung my head, and took a few deep breaths.

The game had been a disaster. A few times Christine had been open in our forward half, but I always misjudged which direction she was going to take, or whether she would slow down or speed up to evade the defence. At one stage during a corner kick she had stepped on my foot. I'd been so steamed I didn't make it back to position in time which had led to an opposition goal. Transitioning the play to our forward line had always been my strength. I couldn't get it together today and we had lost.

"Everyone," Naomi said. "Before Coach gets in here I want to say some things. That was just one game. One. We can bounce back and win the whole damn comp from here. Champions don't let setbacks knock them on their ass!"

A flicker of hope lit the oppressive darkness in my chest. I took another deep breath and tried to keep my voice steady. "Yeah, we can see this as an opportunity to learn from our mistakes."

"You better be talking about *your* mistakes."

Silence descended with a *whoomp*. Everyone looked at the speaker.

Christine. Of course.

I stood and rounded on her. My hands were shaking. Blood was pounding in my ears.

She stood too.

Naomi stepped in between us and held up her hands. "Hey, hey, hey now. Keeley's not the only one who made mistakes. We live and die as a team, yeah?"

"I don't see how were going to *learn* from our mistakes if we don't shine a spotlight on them. I would never have let Number Six past me if McGee hadn't yelled nonsense at me about running at her. Plus," she raised her chin. "My mistake didn't cost us a goal."

Now my blood roared in my ears. Never in my life had somebody come at me so aggressively. "You don't think I already feel bad enough? I own my mistake, but it wouldn't have happened if you hadn't been fucking whining about some shit after the corner!"

Her eyes widened. "Sure, so your loose checking is my fault now? That's a goddamned joke, McGee!"

"You've taken every opportunity to piss me off since you got here. And why? You're a bad apple. Bad for the team!"

Her voice rose to match mine. "There's one person in this room that lost us that game, and it sure as fuck isn't—"

"Keeley, Christine! What in hell's name is going on in here?" Coach was standing in the doorway. Silence fell with an even bigger whoomp this time.

I snapped my mouth shut. I got a flash of what Coach must have just walked in to see—me in my bra screaming about apples and throwing my arms around. I ran my hand down my face. My cheeks were red-hot.

This is not me! I had never let anyone get to me so bad. And right then it seemed like she might cost me everything.

Chapter 4

2023

Back in Melbourne I didn't get much of a reprieve from Viv's telling off before the Australian Women's National team coach phoned me.

Megumi Nishikawa hadn't got the top job by doling out niceties. She cut straight to the point.

"I know raising the profile of women's soccer in the mainstream media was one of our measurable objectives for this World Cup campaign, but this was not what I would call a success."

"Yes, Coach. Sorry, Coach."

She asked me whether I'd been drinking the night before. I hadn't.

"And no drugs?"

"Of course not."

She didn't press the point. We were drug tested regularly under international football federation rules, so there would be no point in me lying to her.

"Keeley, I know we set high standards for the squad, and I know this must be difficult at times—strict diet, a training regime, in bed before midnight—"

"I was in bed before midnight," I said, then straight away winced and slapped my hand to my forehead.

Coach let the silence draw out. She didn't have to say that "in bed" didn't mean "in a hotel room with a popstar you just met."

The conversation got worse from there. It seemed that the Australian soccer governing body was getting calls from journalists and had to come up with something to say.

"You haven't broken any team rules, and we won't slap you with a sanction for bringing the game into disrepute because you technically haven't done that either. So, your punishment is just a warning from me. And here it is—the next time you think about doing something that might embarrass the team, just don't do it. Okay? The World Cup is coming up fast, and distractions are not a good thing. So, what's that Australian term I like…keep your head in?"

"Pull your head in."

"That's it. Pull your head in, Keeley."

The call went on for a few more minutes. Coach didn't raise her voice at all, which somehow was way worse than being yelled at. "You may not want to believe it, but I want what is best for you, and everyone else in the squad," she said. "It's a coach's job to know what the best thing is, even if the players don't know it themselves. So give me a little bit of trust."

"Yes, Coach."

"And do exactly what I say from now on. No distractions. Keep it simple."

After I had apologised more than a dozen times and we'd hung up, I felt sick to my stomach.

Someone cleared their throat. Viv and Fletch were poking their heads around the kitchen doorframe like naughty kids out of bed late at night.

"What's the verdict?" asked Fletch.

"Not kicked off the team, thank goodness. I got off with a warning." I exhaled. It felt like I'd been holding my breath all afternoon.

Viv skipped over and gave me a big hug. "Oh, I'm so glad! I bet the only person who isn't happy is your understudy. You nearly breaking your legs on that bin might have been her big break."

I rolled my eyes and grinned. "It doesn't work like that. We don't have understudies in soccer."

"We've got subs, though," said Fletch. "That's the same, right?"

I shook my head. "I'll never win if you keep ganging up on me. This has been the longest day of my life. I need a cup of tea so strong I can stand a spoon up in it. Anyone else?"

There were no takers so I made my cuppa and sat on a lawn chair in our tiny yard. I closed my eyes and lifted my face to the golden sunshine.

Soccer coaches had helped me so much over my life, but my current Matildas coach had unknowlingly screwed me over months before. She'd e-mailed me when the World Cup draw had been announced and we found out we were in the same group as the US. She sent me a video file of Christine's best plays with the US team and her Seattle team, Reign. More than three hours of Christine—gliding over the grass like a hummingbird. Pulling off super-human feats of skill and agility. Holding her arms up and smiling gracefully at the crowd after she scored.

I sighed and squeezed my eyes shut tighter. Christine's fluid movements played behind my eyelids as a bright, neon shape, leaving a slight trail behind it.

There had been nights back in college where I would fall asleep thinking about her then have her in my mind when I first woke up. But this was different, of course. Back then I was fighting not to think about her. Now, a slight but commanding Japanese soccer coach had explicitly instructed me to study Christine and commit her to memory. The fate of my team and a fair amount of national pride was on the line.

After today's drama it should have been Amber who filling my mind, not Christine.

But that was the thing about Christine. She was difficult and unpredictable. She never went with the flow. Strong—like an unexpected minor note in a familiar tune. But often it was the challenging counter-melody that made a song stick with you, maybe forever.

I smiled as I reached for my cuppa. One night with a singer-songwriter and I was waxing lyrical in my backyard.

I really needed to pull my head in and figure out why I seemed to spend half my time pissing off coaches I admired and respected. The late-autumn Melbourne afternoon was mild, but I shivered at a memory of a different afternoon, also in autumn, after my first game with Christine in Charlottesville.

Chapter 5

2019

Coach had walked just the two of us out onto the deserted pitch once we'd both cooled our heels after our altercation. She rounded on us. Christine sucked in a sharp breath beside me.

"Two things happened today that I will not permit to happen again. One I can help you with and one I can't. The first—a complete communication breakdown on the pitch. In all my years in this job I have never seen two of my players so at odds for an entire game. Mistakes happen, but what I'm disappointed in is that I didn't see an effort from either of you to turn it around."

My stomach plummeted. She was right. I prided myself on my on-field leadership, but today I had let everyone down.

"I won't even address that display in the rooms. Are either of you in *any* doubt about whether that was the behaviour I expect from my senior players?"

"No ma'am," Christine said.

"No, ma'am," I echoed.

"Good. This…off-field business between the two of you needs to get sorted out," she said waving her index finger back and forth between the two of us. "You're on your own with that."

I nodded and pressed my lips together. I had already made a plan for this: minimise contact, pretend she didn't exist, don't let her get under my skin.

"As for the on-field business, that I can help you with," Coach continued. She folded her arms. "We host Duke in two weeks. Every evening until then you are going to have an extra session together, just the two of you. You're going to run drills and practice skills until you know each other's games inside out."

Shitballs!

"I really don't think—" Christine began, her voice forceful and high.

Coach cut her off just by lifting her hand. "Ladies," she lowered her chin. "I didn't plan on telling you this, but the college's selection panel was against my plan to bring Christine over from Northwest so late in her education. I got them over the line by convincing them the transition play between you two would be a gamechanger for us. I'd studied your play, Christine, and was so sure your style would fit seamlessly in with Keeley's. I convinced them all it was a good idea." She looked steadily into my eyes then Christine's. "I've got a lot riding on this, so don't let me down." She clapped us both on the shoulder then stalked off toward the rooms.

My arms swung limp at my sides and my brain wouldn't make thoughts. Christine stared at me with her jaw clenched before turning on her heel and following Coach.

I stomped on the dampening grass. "Yeah, well, I'm not happy about it either!" I muttered. I had wanted to scream it, but didn't want Coach to rouse on me again.

I hunched my shoulders and trailed after them.

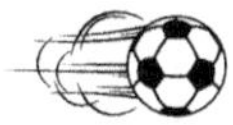

Beyond the floodlit pitch at Florida State University, darkened playing fields spread out into the inky night. I shivered. It was the middle of the night and I only had my arch-enemy for company.

"This is inhumane!" I said. My voice was thin and high. "I have an exam in the morning."

"The sooner we get to it the sooner we'll get through it." Christine ran to the bag of balls on the halfway line and tossed me one, perfectly executing the sideline throw-in technique of course. I gritted my teeth. *Inhumanely stranded here with this inhuman Little Miss Perfect.*

"Rhyming about it isn't going to make it any better, you know," I said as I caught the ball and stalked back to the start point of the made-up, pointless drill.

"Well it could hardly be any damn worse, could it?" she called from across the pitch.

I scowled. With anyone else this kind of ribbing would have been fun. But enjoyable banter requires your adversary to have at least one shred of humour in their being.

Still scowling I began to dribble up the pitch again. Christine made her break. *So fast.* But she was slowing. She propped on her right foot. She was going to come toward me. I fired a bullet pass short, just as she peeled off toward the corner. The ball flashed behind her and trickled over the line. She threw her head back and groaned. I let out a growl too, and ran to fetch the waylaid ball.

"Don't huff and puff at me! How was I meant to know you were going to run away and make your angle worse?" I said.

"You're the one huffing and puffing! And why would I run to the centre, where Duke's entire defence will be hanging out? You know they zone high and guard space."

I bit back a retort. She was right. I did know that about Duke.

Christine cocked her head. "Look." She jogged up and stood next to me. "Picture how this would play out. You've either got an intercept, or you've beaten one of them for possession, and our whole team is streaming into attack. Duke are freaking out, but they keep it tight because they're well drilled. What happens next?"

I looked over my shoulder, picturing myself streaking up the sideline. My head turned slowly as I followed the imaginary me's path.

"Ummm, their winger and at least one of the defenders tries to cut me off." I pictured Duke's white-and-blue uniform.

"Right, and then?"

"The redhead who wears the blue headband holds the middle and…" I closed my eyes. "If I peel out to my right, I draw two more." My eyes snapped open. "If I fake out redhead even one step I'll create a hole behind her. You're the only one quick enough to be there in time, but if I land it right on you, you can either trap it or head it right past the goalie!"

"Exactly, and think of the angle if you kick on your left."

I closed my eyes again. "Oh, ripper! Wrong-foot the whole lot of them." I opened my eyes.

Christine was grinning.

I was too.

"Yes, well." She dropped her eyes. "You have to pull it off first. Let's go again." She pointed to my start position.

"Yes, thank you, I know where it is. I've run to that spot fifty bajillion times tonight." I kicked the ball harder than I meant to and it overshot the target. Running to fetch it I tried to tamp down on a flash of annoyance. Christine was maddening! The first time we'd managed an exchange that wasn't catty enough to make it onto the *Real Housewives of Tallahassee,* and she had to shut me down like I'd said something offensive.

Nope! I had resolved to not let her get under my skin. Her acting like a normal human being for ten seconds had made me lower my guard, but I was stronger than this.

I stood ready to start our torture drill again and took a deep breath. I scanned the playing field in front to me, conjuring Duke's lines of defence. I pictured a turnover deep in our back line, the ball shooting out to me. I took off running. My make-believe crowd cheered in stereo as the field opened up and Duke scrambled to get back.

Christine blew off her tagger with sheer speed and sprinted forward. The goalie came a few paces out but changed her mind and held position. Blue-banded redhead cut off every angle by plonking herself front and centre, just as her coach would have told her to do. But I held, fading slightly toward the sideline to make a defender run off-course. Redhead moved to cover me. The goalie moved one pace to her left. At that exact moment Christine cut a graceful arc right to the goalie's blind spot. I stopped short, tapped the ball with my right foot then launched with my left. Christine didn't break stride as she trapped it at her collarbone, then, without even letting it bounce, drilled it with her right foot into the back of the net.

"Oop, there it is!" I yelled. She gave a double fist pump toward the imaginary grandstand. I had never been happier at a fake goal in a training drill. Christine caught my eye, lifting her chin and dropping her hands.

I was tempted to point out that I had seen her demonstrating happiness and there was no way she could deny it, but I decided I didn't want to antagonise her.

"Let's go again." She pointed toward my start point again. "This time cut inside before you give it off to me. See where that sends their left-flank winger."

I trotted back without a word, thinking that "hot and cold" was not the right way to describe her. More like, "very cold with the faintest fleeting glimpse of luke-warm, but only very rarely."

Six mornings later I lay awake, staring at the ceiling of my dorm room. The days had been getting shorter and it was still dark at 6:30 a.m.

Viv's phone alarm commenced a very loud rendition of Barbra Streisand's *Don't Rain on My Parade.* She sat up, yawned and gave a full arm stretch like a Disney princess that had just been woken by twittering bluebirds. Then her face glazed over and she started a one-shouldered syncopated dance to the beat of her alarm.

She sang along.

I groaned, reached across and tapped the Off button on the phone on the bedside table between us.

"Ugh, it's way too early for Fanny Brice energy," I said.

Viv's large eyes widened and her mouth swung open to form a silent reproach. She snapped it shut. "How come you're awake this early? *You* don't have to catch a ride to Gainesville to paint sets for a community theatre production of *Fiddler on the Roof.*"

"I sure don't."

"Then why such an early bird?"

"I couldn't really sleep. It's hard to wind down from these late sessions with Christine. I keep replaying a corner kick manoeuvre she came up with. I don't think the angle quite works but she's so hard to argue with when she's sure of something."

"Hmm."

"What?"

She leaned her elbow on her pillow and rested her chin on her hand, lips pressed together in a little grin. "Well…what if—and just go with me here—what if I told you there was someone I lay thinking about first thing in the morning. What would you say?"

I narrowed my eyes. "I can see where you're going with this, Vivienne—"

"And what if I told you they were the last thing I thought about every night as I lay drifting off to sleep?"

"What? No way! I do not think about Christine Delacourt in bed at night!"

"Really?" She sat up in bed and cocked her head. "You were sleep-kicking at midnight. I had to roll you from your side to your back. Who were you kicking it to, pray?"

I tossed my pillow at her. "You're full of shit, you know that? Anyway, it's not my fault Christine's been on my mind every so often—I've been forced against my will into close proximity with her for hours on end. I must have a bit of, you know, that thing? Stockholm Syndrome."

Viv inhaled sharply and she grinned. "You mean the thing where people fall in *love* with their captors?"

"Gah! That's not what that is. They just start to feel, you know, an affinity for them."

"Aww. Affinity? Is that what you're going to name yours and Christine's first baby? Can I be godmother?" Her phone pinged and she reached for it. "Caspian's ten minutes away."

"Quick! You can't go to the community theatre until you get dressed all in black and put on your beret."

"A timely interruption. Just your luck." She jumped up, scrambled around for clothes and her toothbrush then rushed out the door to the bathroom down the hall. After a second, she poked her head back around the doorframe. "But this isn't over, McGee. Oh no. Not by a long shot." She closed the door.

I counted aloud. "One, two, two and a half, thr—"

The door opened again. "Oh, I forgot to wish you a *love*-ly day. I'm going to *love* hearing about it when I get home." She bid a hasty retreat.

I lay back down in the grey silence and recalled a hazy dream from the night before—Christine running across the field in front of me, her feet barely touching the turf. The curving angle of the perfect pass appeared before me as a golden shimmering line. I kicked but the ball was on a thick stretchy string like one of those cheap paddle ball novelties in five and dime stores. I could hear Christine calling out my name. I kicked again and again.

No wonder I'd woken Viv up with my sleep-kicking. But falling asleep thinking about soccer and waking up thinking about soccer was nothing unusual for me. I scoffed. Viv couldn't be more wrong. I didn't love Christine Delacourt. I didn't even like her!

I rolled onto my side and shut my eyes. I needed sleep if I was going to get through two lectures and a tutorial on media laws and regulation. Then soccer training, followed by my Christine session. She'd said she'd seen a kick-off play Chelsea Football Club had tried in the Women's Super League that had got them a goal within the first twenty-five seconds of a game, and thought we might be able to try it out. And she'd nodded when I described a manoeuvre I wanted to try that Olympique Lyon had pulled off on the weekend. Carved them right up the middle. I'd been pleased with the nod. It was better than a sneer.

Ok, I'm doing it again. I slowed my breathing and instead thought about the drive my family took every September to Gympie to visit relatives. Mount Beerwah out the car window on the left and Wild Horse Mountain on the right. The big Steve Irwin billboard then Buderim, then a stop at Nambour for salad sandwiches with too much grated carrot.

Viv was dead wrong about *why* I was thinking about Christine. But it might not be a bad idea to think about her a little less.

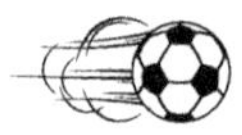

Nearly two weeks later I trained the house down at team practice. Ran all my sprints to the end, was laser focussed on all my passes, and kept up a constant stream of encouragement to everyone around me.

Afterwards Coach pulled Christine and me aside. "Great work out there tonight, ladies. The team's looking cohesive. I'm happy. I've decided tonight can be your last night of detention together. I need you rested and sharp for Sunday's game."

"Oh," I said. I could start going to bed at a reasonable hour again, but I felt a little twinge like something had been taken away from me. I'd thought we had a handful of our little one-on-ones left.

"'Oh?' That's all I get? I thought you'd be turning cartwheels. Anyway, no homework from me tonight. Just keep, you know, getting to know one another's games. Whatever you're doing's working. See you tomorrow." She tossed Christine the keys and went to pack up with the rest of the team.

Christine looked at me and raised her eyebrows.

I gave a little one-shoulder shrug, and was about to say something to acknowledge that the one-on-one session we were about to start would be our last one.

But Christine took a swig of water then slapped the pop-top lid down. "Let's get to it."

I grinned ruefully as I jogged in her wake to the middle of the pitch. "Right you are."

Two hours later, I ran to the sideline for a drink and checked my phone.

"Holy shitballs it's ten thirty!" I called out.

"Oh jeepers! I've got an early lecture."

I pressed my lips together to hide a smile. Sometimes she used funny, old-fashioned turns of phrase. I had grinned once when she'd described something good as "the cat's pyjamas," and gotten a glare for my trouble, so I now tried hard not to react when something tickled me. There was just something about Christine looking like she'd stepped out of a Reebok advertisement in *Cosmopolitan* but talking like a side character in *Grease.*

We changed our cleats for slides, and pulled on our tracksuits. Fall had started in earnest, and northern Florida was a lot cooler than where I was from.

We slung our kit bags over our shoulders and walked together to the light tower that housed the switch. Christine deftly unlocked the little hatch and hit the first switch that shut off half the lights. Every other night I'd wait for her—because it would be a jerk move to leave her alone on an almost deserted playing field in the middle of the night—and look longingly up toward my dorm building and think of a hot shower, a microwave meal and my comfy bed. But tonight I watched Christine. Her movements were so economical and precise.

I felt a pang in the middle of my ribcage. Just a faint one. And it wasn't anything connected with anger or hurt that she hadn't acknowledged that this would be the end of our extra time together. It was simpler. I would miss spending time with her.

The rest of the floodlights shut off with a clunk high above our heads, plunging us into inky blackness. I heard Christine's footsteps in the grass. My heart jumped. I couldn't tell how far she was from me. It crossed my mind she might walk right up to me and there would be no space between us at all.

My eyes adjusted and allowed the faint glow of a nearby streetlight to illuminate us. Christine was a few steps away, looking over her shoulder at me, probably wondering why I was standing with my feet rooted to the spot and my palm pressed to my chest. I dropped my hand and followed her.

"You okay?" she asked as we reached the ring-road that was the boundary to the campus proper.

"Yeah, um, just tired all of a sudden. These extra sessions have been a killer."

"Oh," she replied.

I looked at her quickly. "Uh, I didn't mean… I just meant getting to bed late and less time to study has been tough. The sessions have been, you know…we've made a lot of progress."

She nodded.

We reached the path where I usually went right and she went left to her dorm. Tonight though she headed up the right-hand path without stopping.

"I'll walk you to your door. You looked a little woozy back there."

"Thanks." That pang in the middle of my chest was back. Maybe it was good she stuck with me—maybe the feeling had been a subtle precursor to a severe cardiac episode.

The campus was not deserted nearer the dorms. There were a few people returning late (or early, depending on your point of view) from the Tallahassee bars that were within walking distance.

We walked for a while in silence.

"Hey," I said. I had started talking because I felt the sudden need to acknowledge the shift that had occurred between us, but I hadn't decided what I was going to say. *I don't hate you anymore.* That sounded mental. *Thank you for not being mean to me anymore. It's nice.* The silence yawned out between us.

I cleared my throat. "What time's training tomorrow?"

"Six o'clock."

"Yep, okay." The same damn time as every other Thursday training session this semester!

We trudged in silence a minute longer. Had it always been this long of a walk to my dorm? Finally we reached the glass doors with the welcoming fluorescent lighting inside.

"Well, this is me," I said, clicking my fingers and pointing with both hands to the door.

"Uh-huh." We stood still for a second. I'd never met anyone more willing to let a silence sit rather than fill it with pointless noise.

Her lips twisted the very slightest amount. A couple of weeks ago I either wouldn't have noticed or would have interpreted the movement as displeasure. But I knew better now. Amusement. Faint.

My heart started doing that racing thing again. She had walked me to my door and we now stood face to face, for all the world like a 1950s couple that had just gone on a date to the roller rink then the diner for chocolate shakes. Suddenly all my skin was burning at once, and I wanted to crawl out of it. My eyes flicked to hers for just a second. The amusement vanished, like a roller door had been slammed down. My skin stopped burning and there was a coldness in its place.

"I'll see you tomorrow," Christine said, hoisting her kit bag higher on her shoulder and walking off.

"Bye." Without thinking I turned so I could watch her walk away down the well-lit concrete path. The strange coldness intensified.

I sighed, suddenly struggling to keep my eyes open. Hot, cold, heart palpitations—I was going to need to take some Advil before bed. I didn't need this compounding exhaustion to turn into the flu.

What a weird night.

Chapter 6

Coach was upbeat at the half-time break of our big game against Duke and told us to keep attacking. We'd come close to scoring a few times, but the score was still nil-all. Our team huddled up on the pitch before second-half kick-off. Christine was next to me. After Naomi's gee-up speech Christine didn't run off right away but stayed with her arm around my shoulder.

Okay, I'm not complaining at all about this. I left my arm where it was too, slung down her back with my hand resting at her opposite hip.

She squeezed my shoulder and spoke low into my ear, "We got this, yeah?"

I nodded. "Yeah."

She jogged away. I sprinted into position and again took a moment to myself. I tried to take in the cool breeze on my face, the smell of french fries, and the sound of the crowd. But I couldn't hold on to any of it. Instead all I could feel was a lingering pressure on my shoulder from Christine's hand and the feel of her body through her jersey against my palm. I closed my eyes and breathed deep.

My awareness shot across the pitch to where she was, as if I was trying to home in on her energy. I decided not to fight it. I needed to channel my strength for the game, not in trying to fight against my own brain. I pictured her—focussed, poised, ready to fight. My eyes flicked open. As I looked at her standing at the halfway line it was like everything else blurred into the background.

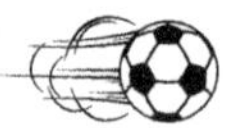

Okay, time to get rid of it. There were only a few minutes left in the game and I found myself with the ball in our forward half. I looked ahead. Three people ahead of me—none other than redhead-blue-headband and Christine, plus Duke's big goalie. Christine was running at full tilt. And not a normal person's full tilt, more like insanely fast. And readhead-blue-headband was keeping pace. Big Goalie had all her weight going forward, focussed on the pair running straight at her.

I bunted the ball in a very ungainly way so it stopped short a few feet to Christine's right. She cut back inside just as the ball left my foot, leaving her opponent flailing in her wake. Big Goalie, eyes wide, desperately tried to get across to cover. Christine planted her left foot and pivoted delicately, spearing the ball in behind the goalie. The net billowed out like a sail lofted by a stiff breeze.

The crowd's roar came into focus and filled my head. I realised I was roaring too, both fists clenched in front of me. I ran forward. Christine ran toward me with her arms outstretched, grinning. She put her hands on my shoulders and jumped. I lifted her and held tight around her waist to keep her aloft.

"Wooooo hoooo," she yelled, and the crowd roared louder in response. I let her slide down. I expected her to let go, but she held both arms tight around my shoulders and pressed her forehead against my cheek and jaw.

"We fucking did it," she said softly.

I swallowed hard. "Yeah." I was surprised any sound came out at all. My throat was tight and I struggled to catch my breath. I was hyper-aware of two things—my arms wrapped tight around her ribcage, and her face against mine. Her breath tickled my neck. I held her a little tighter. If I didn't let go I could feel it again. And again.

Our teammates crashed into us, whooping loudly. Christine and I let each other go as everyone got around us for high-fives. It felt like the whole team ruffled my hair. They weren't game to muss up Christine's though.

"Okay, focus up. Let's go again and get another." Coach's voice sounded above the crowd.

I started to enjoy myself then. Duke still pressed hard, but their precision tactics got a bit ragged as the pressure of needing to score took its toll. After a few minutes Renee attempted a long cross from the sideline to one of our mids, but Renee's ball actually bent and looped down impossibly to sneak into the top corner for a goal. I laughed with delight as I ran to congratulate her.

She was shaking her head and repeating "total fluke" again and again as we mobbed her.

"Just claim it. Pretend it was on purpose. I heard there might be a scout from Orlando Pride here," Christine said.

I grinned and slapped Renee on the back, but I was looking at Christine. Kindness looked good on her. My chest swelled.

When the game finished not long after, I clapped my hands above my head to thank the crowd for cheering us on. Hundreds of faces beamed back at me, grinning and clapping, some calling out to me by name.

I jogged into the middle of the pitch to shake hands with the Duke girls and high-five and hug my teammates. I looked around for Christine and ran over when I spotted her. She gripped my hand and slapped me on the back.

"Great game," she said. She smiled but her eyes didn't meet mine.

"Yes. You too," I said. She jogged past me.

I pressed my lips together. It was nuts to have a sinking feeling in my gut just after one of the best wins I'd ever had. I shook my head and gave my hands a little shake for good measure.

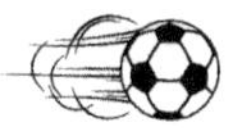

"Here she is, my conquering hero!" Viv pulled me into a big hug.

I'd had dinner with the team at a cheap and cheerful Italian restaurant, but it was mine and Viv's tradition to get ice cream sundaes together after home games—win or lose. Our usual place, Barney's Diner, served the biggest and best sundaes in Tallahassee. It was also open 24 hours, which was crucial because Coach's post-match post-mortems could go on for ages. She'd kept us so long at dinner that I arrived for dessert after 11 p.m.

I sat down on the cushioned bench seat of the booth with a quiet grunt. I shifted my bum along the bench by degrees, wincing each time, so I could lean my head against the wall.

Viv arched her eyebrows. "And you call *me* a drama queen."

I glared at her through one slitted eye, but couldn't think of a comeback. Instead, I held my hand out across the table and she reached over and squeezed it. "You're an ace friend for coming to the match," I said. "Did you have the original cast recording of *Little Shop of Horrors* on your headphones?"

"Surprisingly close. *Rocky Horror Picture Show.* My callback for Magenta is tomorrow." She picked up a sachet of stevia and studied it closely, then glanced at me. "I liked the scene where you did that long kick to Christine and she kicked it into the goal. I saw the goal celebration too."

Our sundaes arrived.

"Oh boy, oh boy, how good does this look!" I plunged my spoon in and took a big bite. I looked over my shoulder at the door, then across at the novelty licence plates on the far wall, anything to avoid Viv's probing gaze.

She cleared her throat. "I didn't think you were going to let her go."

"Who?"

Viv scoffed.

I placed my spoon down. "All right, all right. Uhhhhhh." I scrunched my face up. "I think…I like Christine."

Viv balled her little hands up into fists and pressed them to her cheeks. "As in *like* like?"

I nodded, opening up one eye but still wincing. "Like like. I fancy her."

She leaned over the table and slapped my shoulder. "Oh my goodness, so exciting! You two are just like Scarlett O'Hara and Rhett Butler."

"I don't know who those people are."

She gave a long and loud gasp. "Heavens! What are you going to do next? When are you going to tell her?"

"Whoa, whoa, whoa. Calm the farm for a second. I'm not going to do anything at all about it."

She looked so pained that she could have been mistaken for one of those old-timey tragedy masks. "Oh but you have to!"

"Why, so my life can play out like some melodramatic stage production for your entertainment? No way. She hasn't given me the slightest sign that she likes me back. I'm not talking about romance. She's never given me any indication that she even likes me as a human being."

"But you told me she'd stopped going out of her way to antagonise you."

"Yeah, exactly. And that's what makes it so pathetic. A girl goes from treating me like total shit to a bit less shit and I fall for her? She'd think I was a nutcase! And maybe I am." I slumped down in my seat.

"Awwww." Viv dragged my arms onto the table and started rubbing my forearms vigorously.

I closed my eyes then opened them after a second. I was actually kind of comforted. I picked up my spoon and took another bite of my sundae. "Plus, did you see how she blew me off after the game?"

"Yeah, that was pretty icy."

"You know what she said to me? Great game. Great game!"

Viv tsked. "She may as well have slapped you across the face."

"All right, now you're just making fun of me."

"Okay, maybe just a little. Look though, if you're not going to tell her how you feel, what *are* you going to do? Just have a crush and be sad forever?"

I looked up at the ceiling and sighed. "Shit, I don't know. I guess? I'll just clamp down on these feelings until after the NCAA tournament. There's a handful more games, then I'll see her a lot less until graduation." I balled my hands into fists and nodded a few times. "Yeah, this is very doable. Just focus on the soccer. That's what I should be doing anyway."

"You should be disassociating from your feelings for the next couple of months? Look, if you say so. I know I wouldn't be able to, but I support you completely."

I grinned. "You always feel enough for the both of us, anyway."

She smiled back at me. "You say that, but I say you're the still waters that run deep. Maybe I'm the only one who knows just how deep."

My limbs and eyelids all started to feel very heavy at once. I yawned. "Let's just eat. You know how emotions tucker me out."

"I do, sweetie. I do."

We ate in silence for a bit. The rich chocolate ice cream, fudge, and whipped cream wasn't cheering me up as much as it usually did. I wished Christine had never transferred from Northwestern. Ever since she arrived she had complicated my life—first by rubbing me up the wrong way, and now by being a distraction of a different type.

But in the same moment, I wished, illogically, for her to take me in her arms again like she had during the game today. More time with her, more soft smiles, more whispered words.

I dropped my spoon into my thick glass bowl with a loud tinkle. I liked things to be simple. My emotions were running so high that they were in danger of burning me out.

Florida State won the next match and every single one after that. Everything clicked. Christine and I linked up like a well-oiled machine, and every other aspect of team play seemed to click in around us.

We'd earned a spot in the championship match, scheduled for the coming Sunday against Stanford at their home stadium. We'd flown over to the West Coast a couple of days before the game.

On the bus back to the hotel after training Christine was across the aisle from me, in the window seat. She sat with her hands in her lap and her headphones on, perfectly still, looking out the window at the passing palm trees and concrete. An ache spread across my ribcage. A few short weeks ago I'd observed her stillness and calm self-possession and thought it was weird, selfish aloofness. Now I felt like I could almost see the quiet strength radiating off her. It was intoxicating, majestic—sexy.

"McGee, Delacourt," Coach said, standing in the aisle right in front of me.

"Huh?" I snapped my mouth shut. *Oh God.* My mouth had been hanging open! Christine took off her headphones.

"The hotel just called. They've upgraded two of the rooms from four-bed to twin. With a balcony and views of the ocean. I'm taking one and I'm putting you two in the other. You'll have more of a chance of being well rested in a more comfortable room. I need you both sharp for the match."

This was bad. I couldn't risk this type of distraction just before the biggest game of my life.

"But, Coach," Christine said. "Keeley snores."

I was about to protest, but snapped my mouth shut again. Christine's complaint might get me back in my usual room and out of this jam.

"Nonsense. She usually rooms with Claire who is the biggest complainer on the team, and I've never heard of this snoring before." She pointed her finger at each of us in turn. "I've made my decision. And a thank you wouldn't go astray, by the way."

"Thank you, Coach," we said in unison as she swayed her way to the front of the bus.

I stared wide-eyed at the seat in front of me. *Just my luck!* I glanced across the aisle. Christine had her headphones back on and was sitting in the exact same position as before—still and upright. She seemed to be unaffected by the change in circumstances that had me so shook. But I knew her better than that.

The sweep of her jaw just below her ear was so tensed that it almost bulged. She was pissed.

Coach kept the senior players, Christine and me included, in a meeting in the hotel's conference room until after 9 p.m. When it was done the two of us went up to our room.

"This is nice," I said. They were the first words either of us had spoken since we left the others. The room wasn't much bigger than what we were used to, but they'd put a little sitting area in one corner and big glass doors led out onto a balcony. Beyond was inky blackness, but the blinking lights of distant buoys indicated we were looking out onto the vast Pacific Ocean. I dumped my bags down and slid the door open. I crossed my arms and leaned on the railing, taking big breaths and relishing the feel of the cold breeze on my face.

The Pacific was my ocean. I'd grown up next to it in Australia and it felt familiar. I was usually too busy to feel homesick, but right then I felt the pull of my family from the other side of the sea. It would be summer there. I couldn't do the maths to figure out exactly what time of day, but there was a good chance my parents were walking along the Moreton Bay foreshore at that very moment.

"I'm going to go out for a bit," Christine said from behind me.

I turned. She'd stepped out onto the balcony without me hearing.

"Oh, where to?" It was none of my business, but I wanted to know.

She paused. "Um, well, the night before big games I like to get out of the pre-match routine. I just need to be in a space where the other people don't know or care about the game, or the team, or soccer at all. It interrupts, you know, the…" She swished both her hands from right to left in front of her.

I nodded. "The current. The, uh, flow. Well, more like the runaway speeding train with Coach up the front driving."

One corner of her mouth curved up. "Or Keanu and Sandy B all up on that bus in that old movie."

I laughed. "Yeah, totally."

She dropped her eyes but there was no way I was going to. I gazed at the little half-smile still on her face. I had made it happen. My tummy felt full of liquid gold.

"Well," she said, stepping away. "I'll go."

"Okay. Take your jacket."

"Yeah. I won't be too long."

"Here, let me close this so the room doesn't get freezing." I pulled the door shut. On the other side of the glass she compressed her lips and gave a little nod. Of thanks? Maybe just acknowledgement.

After a few minutes I ducked back into the room and grabbed a jacket and a thick blanket that was folded in the closet, then went back out and sat in a low chair on the balcony.

It would be good to copy Christine's idea and go to a coffee shop or diner where no one gave a shit about the NCAA championship. A healthy jolt of perspective. She was smart. And beautiful. And really, really good at soccer.

In what seemed like no time there was a tap on the glass. I jumped. Christine opened the door a crack.

"How did you go?" I asked, my neck craned around in my deck chair.

"Good. I just chilled in the lobby for a bit. I'm going to take a quick shower."

"Okay, nice. Hey, were there any good strangers who didn't care about ball sports?"

She gave the slightest hint of a smile. "One guy in a three-piece suit was arguing on his phone about whether he should use his opera season pass to see *The Marriage of Figaro* or *Rigoletto*."

"I guess even non-sports people like to pick sides."

"I guess. I'll leave you to it."

She glanced out to the ocean blackness before sliding the door shut.

The tips of my toes were starting to feel chilly, but I didn't want to sit in the room and listen to the shower, because if I listened to Christine in the shower, there would be a massive chance I would start to picture Christine in the shower, and that felt pretty wrong without her permission. I snorted. It would be way creepier to actually ask for her permission for something like that.

The faint sound of the bathroom door opening and closing came through the glass. I sighed and stood up. I couldn't skulk out there all night.

She looked up as I opened the door. I grinned. She sat on the edge of the bed arranging things on her nightstand—a hairbrush, her phone, a lip balm—all equidistant and at right angles from each other. But what had tickled me was her get-up.

"Wow, I didn't think anyone wore striped pyjamas anymore. Did you buy them at Colonial Williamsburg?" They were a thick white-and-blue stripe, with full length pants and short little sleeves. The top had big white buttons all down the front.

"Oh, I…" she looked down at her knees.

"Er, sorry. I didn't mean to—I mean, I was just surprised."

"No, it's fine. My grandma in Seattle sends me a pair for Valentine's Day every year."

I wanted to slap my forehead hard with my palm. "Sorry again. They're really nice. I need to stop running my mouth off without thinking."

"Again, it's fine. Anyway, you wouldn't be you if you suddenly developed a filter."

We looked at each other for a beat. Was she insulting me? She didn't smile. But her eyes weren't cold. Shit, even the slightest hint that she was joking with me, teasing me, made my head spin.

"I'm going to have a shower," I said. I grabbed my stuff without a backwards look.

When I came back out, clean and with my teeth brushed, she was sitting cross-legged on her bed. All the lights were off except the lamp next to my bed.

"I'm going to meditate. It helps me sleep before big games," she said.

"All good. I'll read. I've got to finish *Moby Dick* by the end of term for this dumb English Lit elective I'm taking."

"Old Ishmael and the white whale, hey?"

"That's it. Did you have to read it too?"

"No, I just read it for fun one summer."

"Of course you did."

I smiled. I didn't have enough mystique to keep her guessing about whether I was being mean or not.

She raised her eyebrow then put her palms up on her knees.

I propped some pillows up behind me, grabbed the almost pristine paperback from the bedside table and held it up in front of my face.

It was no good. The words on the page might as well have been ancient Greek for all the sense they made to me. I gave in and lowered the book, just a tiny bit.

Christine's shoulders in her striped pyjamas rose and fell as she breathed. Her eyes were closed and her lips slightly parted. Her quiet power struck me like a blow to the chest. She was magnetic.

I ran my eyes over her in the low light—where the pyjama top crossed over at the top of her chest, just above the first big white button. I watched as she exhaled through her perfect lips. I breathed in time with her, imagining how it would feel to brush my lips against hers.

I sat as still as she was, letting her wash over me like a wave.

Her eyes flicked open and found mine.

Shit! I wasn't quick enough putting the book back up in front of my face.

I cleared my throat, panic rising. The super-awkward silence stretched out. "I've always wanted to learn how to meditate." The words tumbled out, thin and strangled.

"Oh?"

"Yeah. Yes! Absolutely. Will you teach me?"

Her brow furrowed, and she pressed her lips together. It looked like she was calculating if there was any socially acceptable way to say no.

A couple of months ago she wouldn't have thought twice about shutting me down like a guillotine. This silent reluctance was progress!

"Okay, sure," she said. "Cross your legs and rest your hands on your knees like this. Sit with your back straight and don't lean. Yes, like that. Now close your eyes and breathe slowly and deeply."

I took a few breaths. My heart pounded so loud I was sure she'd be able to hear it.

"Now, there's all kinds of ways to do it, but I just try to concentrate on my breath and the present moment. Let everything else fall away. Let your mind go blank."

Is she still watching me? Or does she have her eyes closed too? Am I breathing too fast?

"If you notice any thoughts cropping up, don't fight it. Just acknowledge them and let them drift away," she said.

She really has a great voice. I wish she'd say something else. Oh no! My face is hot. Am I going bright red? I can actually feel *her looking at me. I can't take it anymore!*

I opened my eyes.

She regarded me calmly. "Well? What did you think?"

"Me? Oh, wonderful—so relaxing. So, you know, peaceful. Thanks so much."

She nodded, then walked in between our beds, standing close to me to turn down her covers. I tensed. To me it seemed like every atom in the room was charged with how much I wanted her. There was no way she could fail to notice it.

She stood still for a second, rolled her neck a couple of times and cleared her throat. Then she got quickly into bed.

"Good night," she said.

I shuffled down to lay my head on my pillows and switched off my bedside lamp.

"Night," I said. It came out like a mouse squeak.

I heard her roll over. I squeezed my eyes shut and tried not to think about her exquisitely muscled legs arranging themselves in the sheets.

I curled up tight on my side—a hot little ball of desire—conflicting feelings pinging around in my skull.

I wasn't going to sleep a wink that night. Hell, it felt as if I might never sleep again.

Chapter 7

2023

"NERVES ARE GOOD. THEY MAKE you sharper," Fletch said. They patted me on the back with both palms then squeezed my shoulders.

I had nerves all right. We were standing alongside the US women's national team in the tunnel, ready for the first match of our World Cup campaign. The tension around us was as real and present as the night air and sounds of tens of thousands of people above us in the stadium. It buzzed.

I nodded, tight-lipped over my shoulder at Fletch. Although they were a constant, calming presence in my life, nothing was going to lower my heartrate at this moment.

The teams were in two straight lines, like kindergarten classes. Fletch stood close behind me. Next to me was US mid, Mikayla Larkin. She stood tall and straight like an automaton, looking straight ahead. Her thick ponytail was almost frighteningly perfect, and her tan shone. A little further up the line stood Claire. She exuded strength as well. A memory flashed of us going to see *The Conjuring 2* in Tallahassee our freshman year. She'd been so scared by it she made us leave halfway through. We'd snuck in and watched the second half of *Bridget Jones's Baby* instead.

Claire had changed. She looked strong. Her shoulders and legs evidenced years of world-beating professional training. Her features were sharper, more well-defined. But my heart warmed as I watched her. We had grown up together in a lot of ways.

I leaned to my right, craning my neck a little. Second from the front of the US line-up I could see an arm, the hand moving smoothly, touching each fingertip to the tip of the thumb in turn—a gentle constant pattern.

I swallowed hard. Her grandmother had taught the movement to her to help calm her down before elementary school maths tests.

Christine.

The booming voice over the stadium loudspeaker reached a crescendo and the crowd noise went from a dull roar to a roar-roar. From my slightly out-of-formation position I saw the head referee walk forward and pick up the match ball from a dark green plinth, then both our kindergarten lines started to move forward in tandem.

But my legs had forgotten how to move. I felt like I was back in college, caught in a downhill slide with no control over the effect Christine had on me. My stomach dropped as I remembered where the downhill scramble had landed me: straight over a cliff.

Fletch gave me a whack in the ribs. I winced. They didn't know their own strength when their adrenaline was up. But at least they had jolted me into movement.

We were out under the lights. The crowd was unimaginably loud. So much green and gold—thousands upon thousands of people up out of their seats, yelling at the tops of their voices with sheer excitement.

I turned an ungainly 360 as we walked onto the pitch. With every blink I tried to take a virtual photo with my mind. I would never forget this. Walking out with my national team had been my dream since before I could remember. I had pictured it whenever I needed motivation to push myself—if I had to get up at 4 a.m. on a Melbourne midwinter's morning to go for a run, even though a freezing wind was blowing straight from Antarctica. Or when I had to drink only soda water and lime and leave my own 21st birthday party at 9 p.m. because I had a game the next day. And this moment was worth it.

The teams and refs formed one long line and we sang the national anthems. I joined in the first two lines of *Star-Spangled Banner* before

I realised and bit my lip. They'd made us sing it a lot in college. After *Advance Australia Fair* the crowd noise swelled to a primal roar. People yelled, stomped their feet and threw their heads back and yelled to the night sky.

Our captain, Allie Muir, led us, still in formation, to shake hands one by one with the referees, and then the opposition. US skipper, Summer Ryland, gripped my hand tightly and wished me good luck.

"Ta, mate. You too," I replied before the next in line, Mikayla Larkin, gripped me just as tightly.

Before I had time to realise, Christine had grabbed my hand, let it go a millisecond later and was already halfway past me.

"Have a good game."

I didn't reply. Her eyes had slid across my face like a fallen skater across the ice. She hadn't met my eyes but, rather, had focussed for a millisecond on a point two inches sideways from my left nostril.

I couldn't say anything to the next three of her teammates who wished me well. I had the jarring feeling Christine hadn't remembered or recognised me. Surely not, though?

I was nearly at the end of the production line. I pulled myself together enough to acknowledge the last two American players' kind words. I hoped the few after Christine hadn't thought I was rude. Maybe I'd accidentally intimidated them with my stony silence.

We huddled up and I focused with all my strength on Allie's rev-up. It was riddled with expletives as usual. TV production teams had learned to use a panning shot rather than a close-up of Allie pre-game. You didn't need to be an expert lip reader to know the language was too blue for prime-time. She was from Tenterfield, so rough as guts.

We took formation. Fletch was centre back and I took up my accustomed place to their right in the backline.

The ref's whistle blew, and the crowd noise reached an astonishing level as the US team kicked off conservatively backwards to keep possession.

A part of me wanted to put my hands over my ears but instead I jumped up and down on the spot a few times.

The US passes were lightning quick as they zigzagged around. Players were always there to receive them at the optimal time—no effort wasted and no movement unplanned for. My chest tightened. Shit, they were good. I shook my arms to loosen myself up. We knew the standard they would bring. This is what it was to play against the best.

We pressed up as a team in formation. The opposition took us to the right of field then the left, then picked out a free player at about the midway point. Fletch ran up to block her run, and she immediately passed it way back to the defensive line. It was like the opening of a fencing match, with both teams just dinging our sword-things together and feeling each other out.

But they were learning about us. How far we'd move our defensive press up, how quick we'd cover the ground, any weak spots in our formation.

And what had I learned about them? That they were scary-good, and I was frightened. *Less than helpful, McGee.*

Fletch yelled instructions as usual at the top of their voice, but I couldn't hear a single word. Beyond them at left-back was Ava White. She was scowling fit to burst. Sitting back and waiting to nullify the American attack whenever they decided to launch. It was not how she wanted to spend her evening. She played most of her soccer over in Spain for Real Madrid and at twenty-one was considered one of the best defenders in Europe.

The opposition were drawing us over to her side of the field. I could see it unfolding so clearly that it was like watching it on TV. They would draw us all over then slingshot the ball into the open space on my side of the field. From the corner of my eye I could see Christine starting to make a diagonal run. Shit. If she got on the end of a pass and came past me at full pelt I'd never be able to catch her.

I froze on the spot. She was running toward me insanely fast, becoming bigger and bigger by the second. Just like the slow-mo image in my head, the long pass came across. *Hold the phone.* Something was off. Christine was too close to me and Fletch. Like a flash of yellow light Ava streaked through and intercepted the pass. She ran like a bat out of hell straight through the middle of the field. The Americans were caught on their heels. They'd been ready to move into formation behind Christine and ensure a goal. Now they scampered backwards after Ava, who didn't look like stopping as she cut a swathe through them.

I opened my mouth and yelled incoherent encouragement. I couldn't even hear my own voice over the screaming of the crowd. Allie floated in and hung just onside, one pass to the left of Ava.

Two defenders descended on Allie and the goalie took a half-step over to cover her. Our skipper was so dangerous that she was always on the opposition's radar. Ava's head didn't turn a millimetre. She barely broke stride as she slammed the ball into the back of the net.

I leapt into the air and Fletch wrapped me up in an ecstatic embrace before I'd even landed again. Together we ran up and joined the entire team in whacking Ava on the back.

Her face was steely. "Again," was all she said.

The US kicked off.

This time we pressed up aggressively as a team. We sprinted to try and upset each of their passes.

They kept their cool control though.

After about three minutes it crossed my mind that we were going to be pretty bloody tired soon if we kept this chasing up.

Then the break came. Fletch ran up a little too enthusiastically to block a player receiving the ball in the centre and she was able to get around them. Christine sprinted toward me. A lightning pass hit her about ten metres in front of me. She took the ball and made to run toward goal. The crowd noise notched up another decibel.

But strangely, the noise seemed muted. It was reduced to a hum underneath the clear sound of the ball against Christine's boot, her footfalls, her breath. My left brain knew it was impossible that I was hearing these sounds, but I just went with it. I knew she was going to chop, change and fade toward the sideline.

When she did, I had already taken half a step across and kicked the ball neatly out of bounds. Fletch huffed over and gave me a clip on the back of the head and a slap on the bum—their way of saying I'd done good job. I hustled backwards a couple of steps in anticipation of the throw-in.

Half-time rolled around with no change to the 1-0 scoreline. In the rooms Allie crashed down on the bench next to me.

"You're owning Christine Delacourt, Keeley! Shutting her down left, right and centre. Magnificent to watch."

"Thanks, mate. You're playing a blinder too."

Allie gave a single nod then moved off toward the team physios.

I pressed my hands to my belly and tried to regulate my breathing. My head felt like fish thrashing in a bucket. Christine seemed off her game. Was Ava right that I was outplaying her? A sneaky thought flashed up—was Christine as nervous about seeing me as I was to see her?

I squeezed my eyes shut. *Dangerous and stupid idea.* Less than an hour ago I had thought she had forgotten I existed, or at least what I looked like. But that had been an insane idea, too. I hit my fists against my knees. What was it about this woman that undid me so completely?

Back on the pitch the ref's whistle blew. The play was fast and furious. The US had stepped their intent and aggression up a notch. Maybe their coach had given them a talking-to at half-time that had blistered the paint on the changeroom walls.

Christine wasn't at her best. She had some good moments, but she couldn't quite get her angles and touch right when she kicked into the centre. Unfortunately for us, though, the team had ten other world-class players for us to contend with. At the seventy-minute mark one of their mids made a scorching run down the centre. She pulled off a stunning spin to get around Fletch and was able to score and equalise the game.

Then five minutes later I pulled off a slide tackle from behind on Cam Barker, the star forward for Orlando Pride. Unfortunately the ball went out for a US corner kick. Their fullback got on the end of it with a stunning header and put them in the lead.

We fought hard and had a couple of chances to score but couldn't claw back our lead. When the ref's final whistle blew, we had lost 2-1. I ran to Fletch. I knew they would blame themself for giving up that first US goal. Sure enough they were crouched down with tears streaming down their face.

I hauled them up by their underarms and pulled them into a massive bear hug. "Mate, mate, mate. It's okay. Shh, shh, shh." I rubbed their back and talked calming nonsense to them until they were breathing normally.

I took a moment to find comfort in the big embrace too. I had let myself believe that we might pull off the impossible and beat the US. The news reports would all say we'd done well—that as rank underdogs it was a miracle the game had been that close. But all that would come later. Right now I was in my feelings. I squeezed my eyes tight and let the disappointment wash through me.

Then I took Fletch's shoulders and put my forehead to theirs. "Okay now?"

They nodded.

"Defence fucking sucks sometimes, hey? But..."

They nodded and gave a teary smile as we said our favourite catchphrase in unison. "... at least we're not the goalie."

I slapped them on the back, and we walked over to be good sports and congratulate the Americans. Dozens of handshakes, hand clasps, fist bumps with my own team, the ref, the coaches and the opposition later, my head was spinning.

Someone grasped my hand. "Thanks for the game." That voice! *Christine.*

She was right there in front of me again.

"Yeah." It was such a dumb thing to say, but it was all I could get out.

We stood for a second. She barely looked like she'd taken a brisk walk around the block, let alone played one hundred minutes of high-stakes soccer. Her socks made a perfectly straight line just below her knees.

Meanwhile I had wrenched my socks down so they were hanging loose around my ankles and had tossed my shin guards somewhere. I knew I was bright red in the face and shiny from sweat—because that was how I looked after every game I'd ever played in my life.

Christine's eyes focussed just past my right earlobe. She didn't look directly at me. I swallowed hard. I must have looked a right mess, but that was no excuse for her to blank me. I was an idiot to have to be reminded that she was heartless.

I went to pull my hand away and walk off. But she held onto it. Her eyes flicked to mine and stayed there. Her jaw tensed. She put her other hand on my shoulder and moved her thumb along my collar bone. She applied the tiniest amount of extra pressure and stroked almost imperceptibly back and forth.

My breath caught.

"Keeley," she said, so quietly I had to strain to hear her voice. Her mouth twitched into a frown and she closed her eyes for a second.

With her gaze not on me I felt as if every light in the stadium had been shut off and I was alone and invisible. I squeezed her fingers. *Look at me again.*

"Christine, Christine! A quick interview, please. Delia Horowiscz from ESPN." A loud voice with a very American accent brought me back down to earth.

Christine's fingers slipped through mine and she was gone. Gone only a few metres off to the side of the pitch, but the bright bank of lights on a tall tripod and the large camera trained on her cut her off from me so completely she may as well have been on the other side of sound-proof glass.

"Mac!" A hand wrenched at my shirt from behind and I was pulled toward a huddle my team was forming. We leaned our heads in. I loved this, and sometimes felt a physical high from the energy in these circles. Most of my favourite people on the planet, with their energy fixed on a common goal and purpose. Usually like this—with our collective backs to the criticism and scrutiny that came along with being a professional sportsperson—I felt completely at peace. Usually.

I squeezed my eyes shut tight and tugged at the front of my hair. *Centre. Focus. Be in the moment.*

I opened my eyes and drank in every word Allie was saying. We should be proud; we pulled off a performance against the world's best that we couldn't have dreamt of twenty years ago; we'd elevated Australian soccer and created a legacy that would live on after us.

We were a team full of super-competitive people and the sting of defeat wouldn't disappear with one good speech, but Allie was doing just enough to move us forward to focus on the next game against Denmark.

"Now get out there and take some bloody selfies with some fans! People have flown from all over to come see you, and we gave them a fucking ripper performance!" she said.

I threw my arms around Fletch and Ava on either side of me and gave them a squeeze just before the huddle broke up.

I was all in, here, with my crew. Underdogs who had taken it up to the world's best and not disgraced ourselves. I looked up at the night sky, the stadium lights whiting out any chance of seeing the stars. There was a pull from my chest over to where the US team was greeting a big group of supporters wearing the red, white and blue.

I jogged over to the opposite sideline where I reckoned my parents and cousins were sitting. I buzzed with adrenaline, pride, and disappointment. But underneath it all was something else. More than a feeling—it was a force. Christine. I brushed my fingers against my shoulder where I could almost still feel her touch.

It was crazy to let a handshake, albeit a lingering one, in front of thousands of people, flip my centre of gravity sideways. But she had always been able to hold me in place and throw me off balance, all at once.

Chapter 8

2019

CHRISTINE AND I PLAYED A big part in Florida State beating Stanford in the college championship game. After a party in the hotel lobby that went late into the night, there was an official team photo which meant we had to change back into full, clean kit, much to everyone's grumbling.

After the receptionist who took the photo on his iPhone was satisfied with the final result, the team was allowed to disperse. I started to walk toward the elevator with Naomi, but Coach called out from behind me.

"Keeley, Christine—a word please."

Naomi shot me a look like I'd just been called to the principal's office as I turned back. I caught Christine's eye as we approached the middle of the big, otherwise empty lobby.

"Look," Coach cleared her throat awkwardly. "I wanted to, uh, thank you two for the season you were able to put together. I know that our success is in big part down to the unstoppable transition play you were able to create. Attacking opportunities from the very back line all the way up forward again and again are what wore our opposition down and allowed us to win. I know you two aren't exactly the best of friends, but you were able to put your differences aside and play together exceptionally well. I mean, really well. I would swear you two shared a brain at times. Anyway, uh, thanks." She stuck her hand out toward me and it took me a beat to realise she wanted me to shake it.

"It was an honour to play under you, Coach," said Christine when it was her turn for a handshake. "I learned so much about soccer and about myself this season."

"Yeah, thanks," I added lamely, both admiring and envying Christine's ability to always say the right thing at the right time. The girl was a class act all right.

"Yes, well, get to bed you two. I won't hold the bus for you in the morning you know."

Dismissed, we made our way in silence back to the elevator. As the doors closed, we were enveloped in a silent stillness that was way too heavy to break with small talk.

When we got out on our floor and stepped out, I exhaled audibly. I'd been holding my breath.

"Well," I said as we started to walk down the empty hallway. It would be very strange if the two of us didn't acknowledge what Coach had just said. "What did you think of that?" I shot her a quick glance as we walked along.

She stayed silent.

The thought flashed through my mind that I was going to miss her now the comp was done. She'd been at the forefront of my consciousness for months and months now, and I realised that I was used to her being there. I opened my mouth to express this in some way but at that moment she fumbled with the key card as she tried to open our door. *Discomfort.* I snapped my mouth shut as she finally got the key to work, and we walked into the dark room.

She clicked the lights and strode to the window. Her unease radiated off her. She was trying to get as far away from me as possible. My stomach dropped. Yes, I was going to miss her, but I wasn't going to miss the exhausting emotional rollercoaster she had me on. Maybe some space would be the best thing for me.

"I'm gonna..." I pointed to the bathroom and moved toward it. If she wanted some time to be alone, I would leave her alone.

As I reached the door, I felt her hand in the middle of my back. I stood stock still. Her fingers sent electricity up and down my spine. I couldn't move. I couldn't risk moving this moment forward to some normal place, where she was touching me to get my attention and tell me something innocuous like my phone was buzzing, or my Gatorade had leaked all over the carpet.

But I knew, I *knew*, that wasn't going to happen. Behind me her energy was thrumming.

"Keeley." Her voice was hoarse.

She took a step closer, and her breath warmed the skin below my left ear. As I turned she gripped the back of my shirt so her arm was wrapped around me. Her lips were parted and her breaths were coming heavy. Heat was already coursing through me, but as her eyes met mine, piercing into me with naked desire, the physical warm ache between my legs became so great I inhaled sharply.

Her other hand gripped my shirt at the collar just above my right breast. "Have I got this wrong?" she asked. She stood completely still with her lips two inches from mine. It struck me that we were the exact same height. *Shut up, brain! She's asking if I want her!*

I shook my head. "Nope, not wrong. Very not wrong," I said. The words came thickly.

She kissed me, opening her mouth immediately, catching my bottom lip with a knee-shaking sweep of her tongue.

I groaned as my tongue met hers. It felt like an impossible miracle that this girl—*this girl*—was kissing me, but I also had a strange feeling deep down in my brain that her mouth, her taste, was somehow familiar. Maybe us together was so right that the universe recognised it.

Shit! I had a flicker of fear. I'd never had feelings this intense for a girl before.

My hands floated in midair somewhere in the general vicinity of her body. I was scared to touch her. Maybe it would break my brain.

I curled my hands up into awkward loose fists and rested them on her collarbone.

She smiled slowly at me. "Do you want to touch me?"

I swallowed hard. "Yes."

She took few steps back. My hands dropped to my sides. She took her jersey off, then pulled her sports bra up and over her head. She sat down on the closest single bed.

My breath caught. She bit her bottom lip and squared her shoulders, inviting me to touch her skin, her perfect breasts.

The fear turned from a flicker to a hum in my brain. I felt like I was at the edge of a cliff, and if I jumped I'd be smashed to a million tiny pieces.

But my desire was stronger than my fear. This—what was happening now—was an impossible miracle, and those don't come along too many times in a life.

I knelt in front of her and stroked both my hands across her breasts, nipples dark brown and becoming hard the more I touched them.

"Are you okay? You look like you're about to cry, McGee." She said it gently and I could hear the smile in her voice. I smiled too, and wrenched my eyes away from her boobs to look up at her face.

"Hey, Christine, what's happening?" I asked her. Still smiling she stroked my hair with both her hands.

"I want to fuck you is what's happening. Unless..." her smile faltered for a split second.

"Oh my God I want to fuck you too! Please don't change your mind!" From my kneeling position I knew there was no way it didn't look like I was begging her not to take her body away from me. But I didn't care one bit.

"Well then, why don't you quit gabbing and keep making me feel good?" This time I didn't wait around for a second invitation. I grabbed her waist and scooched her closer to me on the edge of the bed jamming my body between her knees. I touched my tongue against her right nipple and was gratified when it went rock hard and she gave out a little gasp. I moved my attention and mouth to the left nipple and she groaned and opened her legs a little wider to press herself against my chest, which drove me wild. She grabbed me by the collar and I stood up in front of her.

"You're wearing way too many clothes," she said and dragged me toward where she sat on the bed, and pulled my shirt off. Then she snapped the band of my bra. "Off," she demanded.

I took a couple of steps back. A part of me still couldn't believe that this perfect girl had come on to me out of the blue. Her body was telling me that she wanted me, but I felt the need to see it. I ran my fingers over my nipple underneath the bra, never taking my eyes off her face. Now it was her turn for the breath to catch in her throat. She sat forward a bit on the bed.

"Sounds like you're about to cry, Delacourt." I pulled the bra up over my head.

Christine's voice sounded a bit hoarse as she said, "I will cry if you don't get yourself over here."

"Uh-uh-uh," I waggled my finger at her, still mock-teasing. "I make it a rule to never be nude in socks." I sat down on the bed next to her, as close as possible without actually touching her. She took another lingering look at my boobs before we both set about taking off our cleats and socks. I don't think I've ever managed it faster in my whole life.

"Just like the changerooms after a game," Christine said.

"Same but different," I replied and leaned my upper arm against hers. At my touch she put her hand to the side of my face and kissed me hard again.

"Here," I said, jumping up. "I make it a rule to never let my body touch a hotel bedspread."

"Oh, totally. They never change them."

I ran around the other side of the bed and we both grabbed the doona, peeled it off and threw it onto the floor.

She faced me and took off her shorts and undies together, kicking them across the room. I took the tiniest second just to stare at her. To my sudden horror I thought I might start to tear up.

"You're perfect," I told her.

"You're still wearing too many clothes," she said. I slid the rest of my clothes to my knees then let them drop to the floor.

She sat on the edge of the bed, her body turned around to watch me standing on the other side. In the dim lamplight I knelt on the bed behind her and kissed the side of her neck. She put her hand to the side of my face and pulled me closer. I pressed my breasts into her back. She brought her legs up underneath her and knelt high enough to kiss my mouth. Her tongue found mine again and again, and her hand entwined itself in the back of my hair, still holding me tightly to her. With my body still pressed into her back, I slid my hand down her belly and stopped when my fingers reached her short pubic hair. I drew my mouth back from hers.

"Is this okay?" I asked her.

She bit her bottom lip and nodded. I kept my eyes fixed on hers and slid my fingers around her labia. She was wet and swollen. Her breath caught and she started to move against me, the feeling of her firm strong arse against my thighs driving me crazy.

"Is inside okay?" I said hoarsely.

"Oh, God, yes," she said.

As I slid my middle finger inside her, she closed her eyes and threw her head back with a soft moan.

I moved my whole hand back and forth and she thrust against me. She wound both arms behind us both and grabbed my bum, pressing me against her so we were jolting and bumping together.

I took her breast in my left hand and rubbed my thumb against her nipple. It hardened even more and she gave another groan and thrust against my hand harder. I quickly wet my left-hand fingers with my mouth and stroked her nipple again.

She arched her back to press her breast against my touch and thrust her hips even harder and faster. She threw her head back and I pressed my open mouth against her jawline, my breathing becoming faster in time with hers, which came in rhythmic moans of "Oh!" again and again.

When she came she clutched both my hands with hers. The small earthquakes that juddered against my fingers inside her shook her whole body. Then she found my mouth with hers and kissed me slowly.

I wrapped my arms around her and she turned to face me. She slid her hand down between our bodies and brushed my labia with her fingertips. I gasped and dug my fingers into her back. Fucking her had been so hot I was turned on to within an inch of my life.

She smiled and stroked the side of my face. "Well," she said.

I smiled back. "Well, well, well."

"Why don't you lie down. You know, get comfy. Stay awhile."

"Yes, ma'am," I replied.

She pushed softly on my shoulders, manoeuvring me so I was lying on my back. My head was near the foot of the bed and my feet were up near the headboard.

Christine spread my legs and pressed her belly against mine. She kissed my breasts and stomach with a fair amount of slow deliberate pressure.

"Damn, you've got a great body," she said thickly.

My mouth fell open. *She* was telling *me* she liked what I was working with! It was as ridiculous as Britney Spears telling me I was good at dancing or writing long nonsensical Instagram captions.

"Er, um, *hello?* You've got the best body, like, on the face of the planet."

She smiled. "Can I make you feel good?"

I didn't trust myself with the making of the words, so I just nodded so vehemently the whole bed rocked.

She moved downwards, her ribcage then her breast sliding against my pussy. I grabbed the bedsheet and gave an involuntary gasp.

She licked and kissed me with the passionate focus she had when she kissed my mouth and body. Waves of pleasure radiated upwards and I started moaning softly in time with the strokes of her tongue. Her breathing became noisy too and she clutched the sides of my hips, rocking a little as well. Our entwined movements became more frantic. I grabbed one of her hands and my orgasm shuddered through me. She kept her open mouth on me until my shaking subsided, then looked at my hand that held tightly onto hers. She brought it to her lips and kissed my fingers then my palm.

I held my arms out to her wordlessly and she lay her body alongside mine, the wrong way around on the narrow, single bed. I kissed her as she wrapped me up with an arm and a leg into a full-body embrace.

I opened my eyes. "That was as good as the win."

"That was better than the win," she replied.

"Shit, that's what I should have said."

She kissed me on the mouth again, then lay back to consider me, running her forefinger gently down my nose.

"It's probably late. Should we sleep?" she asked.

My limbs felt heavy but at the same time every part of me protested at the idea of her body not being against mine.

I stuck my bottom lip out a little.

She scoffed. "What, you're such an athlete you're not even tired after a massive game? Look, you can sleep in my bed with me if you want. I'd like it. Just let me brush my teeth."

"Fine." I loosened my grip.

She stood up, but before she could take a step I sat up on the side of the bed and clasped her around her middle, smooshing the side of my face into the middle of her back.

I felt another unexpected jolt of desire. Every inch of her felt like strength, and it drove me crazy. I kept a tight hold with one arm but ran my hand across her stomach. My tummy didn't feel like that. Did she do crunches in the evenings instead of watching tv?

"Uhhhh, watcha doing there Keeley?"

"I dunno. Nothing. You said you were going to take care of your dental hygiene. I don't understand why you're not just walking away." I grasped her tighter with both arms. "Bye. Stop hanging around like a bad smell. Girls don't like clingy girls, don't you know?"

She laughed and sat down in my lap, turning so she could link her fingers behind my neck. "You like me, hey?"

"Yep."

"I like you too." She kissed me quickly on the mouth. "Make the bed, will you, dear? I'll be right back."

I gave her one last squeeze then let her go.

Later, pressed along the length of her back, sharing a pillow in the single bed, I listened to her quiet slow breathing. I wanted to run my hands along her body, kiss her, make her smile slowly again as she looked at me. I wanted to watch her pant and moan as she threw her head back in ecstasy at my touch again, and see her body flooded with desire as she turned me on.

I let the feeling wash over me but stayed still so I didn't wake her up. I contented myself with focussing on how amazing it felt to hold her. My knees tucked up against the back of hers, her bum smooshed into my crotch, my arms draped over her, and my fingers loosely entwined in hers. I closed my eyes. My nose rested against the base of her neck.

That terrible Aerosmith song started playing in my head and I didn't fight it. They had it spot on—I didn't want to go to sleep. I didn't want to miss a thing.

A tingle of worry pinged just under my ribcage. I had zero chill with this girl. Sure, I'd had a post-coital cuddly glow with plenty of women before, but this felt different. I was dreading having to leave her tomorrow. If I had my way I would walk around all day clasped to her back like a baby koala. She probably had the core strength to manage it. Then I could sit on her lap on the plane.

Forget zero chill! My level of chill was in negative figures and falling fast.

I brought myself back to the present. *She's here now, you've got her held tight, try to enjoy it.* I concentrated on her body against mine again, thinking how I could stay awake all night reviewing our touch-points. *Knees, bum, hand, crook of the neck. Knees, bum, ha…*

I fell asleep in nine seconds flat.

"I'm not about keeping secrets unless there's a very good reason for it, but is it okay if we don't tell the team about us today?" she asked, standing naked with a toothbrush in her hand the next morning. "You can tell whoever else. I don't want you to think I'm not happy about what happened. I just think it's better not to make this weekend all about us. Did you notice Naomi was acting weird when the hotel took our photo last night?"

"Uhhhhh… I have no idea what you're talking about."

She grinned. "You'll never have to worry about team politics because you're completely oblivious."

"Uh-huh." My eyes were starting to ache from trying to look at every part of her body at once. Right then I was watching her perfectly muscled forearm as she gripped the toothbrush, and thinking about how my tongue had found an unexpected ticklish spot on the underside of her wrist a few hours ago.

She snapped her fingers twice. "Hey, Wandering Eyes Wendy. My face is up here."

I lifted my head ostentatiously and opened my eyes wide, locking on to hers.

She grinned and shook her head. "Remember when the photographer moved you and me to the middle of the group shot? He wanted the stars of the winning goal front and centre? Well, Naomi was huffing and puffing off to the side like a prize bull at a gate."

"I remember. Your sleeve brushed mine when you moved next to me. And you laughed a bit when the photo man made us all say 'winniiiiiing' to get us to smile." I scrunched my face and put my index finger to my temple. "Was Naomi there though? Was anyone? I thought we were alone."

She scoffed. "The whole team, plus Coach, plus a whole heap of hotel staff were there, you goofball."

I stood up from the bed and walked toward her. "And the room was candle-lit and strewn with roses."

She laughed. It was low and melodious.

The sound made me tingle at the base of my skull. I gripped her around the waist and pressed my belly to hers. I spread my legs a little so I sunk down to a height that was shorter than hers.

I looked up at her, both my eyebrows raised. "And there was a cellist playing, wearing a tuxedo and a blindfold."

She threw her head back and gave one sonorous *hah!* I pressed my lips to her neck, tasting the soft skin. She lowered her head and gave a soft gasp.

"Keeley," she said softly. "I'm all minty. Let me go spit."

I groaned and released her.

When she came back, I was sitting on the bed scrolling on my phone. She plonked down beside me and laughed when I immediately flung my phone onto the other bed and slid my arm around her waist.

"Since when did you feel like that?" she asked. "With the rose petals and the violin?"

"Cello. Well, um, it wasn't immediate."

She rubbed the back of her neck. "Yeah, uh, sorry I was kind of mean to you when we first met."

"No, that's fine. I forgive you one hundred thousand per cent. I'm sure I wasn't a treat to be around all the time. But, I guess, when Coach made us do that training just the two of us, by the end—I was sad when we had to stop. Then I asked myself why, and the answer was because I liked you."

"I liked you from the very start."

"What?"

"Yeah, um, when you rocked up late for training that first day, you reminded me of a girl I had a crush on in high school. You know, kind of messy and derpy and—"

I held up my hand. "Whoa, slow up with the compliments! I'll get a big head."

She chuckled. "Yeah, sorry. Well, I thought the last thing I needed was a distraction when I'd just joined a new team. It was easier if you hated me."

I creased my forehead. "And then, you kissed me after we'd won and you didn't have to worry anymore?"

"Wow, no, that sounds awful. So calculating. No, I've learned a lot from this team—from you, actually. I wasn't in a good place when I came here. Remember that first game in Virginia? I was such a see-you-next-Tuesday to you. I was scared of failure, and the game was going to shit, and I blamed you for my lack of focus. Cause I'd been thinking about you. I told myself not to, but I couldn't help it, so you scared me a little."

"You scare me a little too."

"Really? How so?"

The edge of a cliff. Smashed to a million tiny pieces. "Oh, you know, because you're good at soccer and stuff."

She tilted my mouth toward hers with a gentle touch of her finger on my cheek. "What else am I good at?" she asked, leaning in.

"Sex," I said without a moment's hesitation.

She kissed me. "We'll have to be fast if we're going to do this before breakfast."

I wrapped my arms around her shoulders.

"I'm sure the bus driver will make a pitstop at Dunkin Donuts if we miss brekkie. We're the fucking NCAA champions!"

Chapter 9

As the bus drove into campus we caught sight of hundreds of people in maroon and white, cheering and waving flags. At the very front were Viv and half a dozen of her theatre set-painting friends, holding a huge banner that said *Welcome home NCAA Champs!* There seemed to be a collection of uneven smudges as a border around the words. As the bus slowed to a stop beside it I realised they were painted interpretations of each player's face. I grinned.

Christine gave my hand a quick squeeze then let go.

I smiled at her. The smile she gave me back made molten gold melt down the inside of my chest.

The team got off the bus one by one, each giving either a quick wave to the crowd as they reached the door, or a more bombastic celebration. Renee clasped her hands and shook them at either side of her head like a boxing champ. When it was my turn, a very small but vocal part of the crowd piped up with the well-known "Aussie, Aussie, Aussie! Oi, oi, oi!" chant. I beamed. It wasn't classy of me, but I joined in as loudly as anyone.

The roar for Christine, who was right behind me, was the loudest. She had given everyone the fairytale of the spectacular last-second goal that wins the match, and they appreciated her for it. I made my way to Viv, giving plenty of high-fives along the way to people I knew, and also those I didn't. I gave her a big hug then stepped back to admire the banner.

"Wow everyone. This is really something!" I said. "I love the big smile you've given me." I pointed to one of the faces.

Viv craned her neck down. "That's not you, silly. That's Claire. You're here." She pointed at a different wibbly blob, also with a big toothy smile.

"Ohhhhh, of course! Sorry, must be the jetlag."

The team posed for some photos for the campus newspaper, then held up the trophy for a final cheer from the crowd before everyone started to disperse.

Viv came over, rolled-up banner tucked under her arm. There were hugs all round. A lot of the team were glassy eyed from exhaustion, but we lingered over final words and farewells, like we didn't want the crazy ride to be over.

I hugged Christine last, just quickly, then took a couple of big steps back. We stood staring at each other for a couple of seconds.

"Bye," I said. I stretched it out too long. It sounded half like a question and half like a random syllable uttered by a lunatic.

"Bye," she replied. It sounded like an affirmation.

The others had trailed off in pairs and threes.

Christine raised her eyebrows for a second. "I'm going to take a nap. If it's okay with you, can I text you later?"

At my shoulder Viv gasped. Christine smiled and didn't take her eyes off mine. At once I melted and felt a rush of desire. My face started to burn.

She flicked her eyebrows at me again. She was enjoying the effect she was having on me.

"I'm free. That, uh, that will be fine and good," I said.

She nodded and bit her bottom lip ever so slightly. "I'll look forward to it then." She hitched up her bag up on her shoulder and walked away.

I closed my eyes. Shit she was cool. And I was like the school dweeb with suspenders and glasses held together with sticky-tape.

Viv grabbed me by the shoulders and gave me a shake.

My eyes shot open.

"What. The. Hell. Dish. Dish. Dish!" She punctuated each word with a rough jolt either front to back or side to side.

"Geez, quit it! I'm fighting exhaustion and I might yarf on you!"

"Not. Until. You. Tell. Me. What's—"

I tickled her on both sides of her ribcage.

She shrieked and let me go.

I shot a furtive little look over each of my shoulders. There were still a few people milling around, but no one too close. I leaned toward her. She leaned toward me.

I opened my eyes wide and took a big breath in through my mouth. "Me and Christine slept together," I said quietly.

"Eeeeeeee!" Viv pulled me into a big hug. "You like her so much! She likes you too?" she asked with the side of her face smooshed into my hair.

I nodded. "She liked me, but she fought against it, but she still liked me. Then Coach put us in a room together just us. Oof!" Viv had squeezed me tighter.

"Sorry," she said, loosening a little.

"And then at night, after the game, she kind of, put her hand on my back, then asked if she could kiss me."

"Eeeeeeee!"

I jerked away and pressed my palm to my deafened ear.

"Sorry. And?"

I narrowed my eyes. Viv leaned forward on the balls of her feet.

I put the tip of my thumb and finger to my lips and gave a delicate chef's kiss.

Viv beamed. I beamed back. Her big eyes welled up with tears. To my dismay I found mine were too. The emotional tumult of the last few days, the joy of the game and the intense rush of being with Christine broke like a wave over me. I wondered what I'd done in a past life to deserve such happiness.

Viv picked up my bag, wobbled a little at the weight, then threw her arm around my shoulder.

"Keeley, I can honestly say I've never seen you like this about a girl before. Let's get you home for a kip."

I suddenly felt exhausted. Hollowed out.

"Now," said Viv as we set off toward the dorm. "Tell me all about what happened in your grand finale game."

Chapter 10

2023

FLETCH YAWNED, SHOWING EVERY WISDOM tooth. "I'm bushed. I'll turn in."

"G'night," Viv and I answered in unison.

Our next World Cup match was in Melbourne, so they'd let the few of us who lived there sleep at home for a couple of nights. It was a clear, crisp July night and we were having our customary fire-pit time in the back yard.

"Thanks again for dinner, Viv. It was delicious," they said as they went inside.

It had been good—vegan Irish stew. I wasn't vegan but Viv and Fletch both were, so every meal I ate at home, including the ones I cooked myself, was necessarily vegan.

Viv turned in her chair to answer but Fletch had already closed the sliding glass door and was on the other side of it. She blew a kiss instead and gestured flinging it toward them. They grinned and caught it.

"I missed you two ding-dongs. It was creepily quiet here without you," said Viv.

"You watched us on the telly, though, right?"

"Yeah, duh." She took a swig of her mug, looked at it in betrayal because it was empty, then set it down on the grass. "It was funny seeing Christine again."

"Mmmm." I waited, smiling as Viv's right foot started to fidget wildly.

She exhaled loudly through her mouth. "All right, yes, I want to ask you, you hold-out. What was it like seeing Christine again?"

"Yeah, fine. *Oi!*"

She had thrown a balled-up blanket from Fletch's chair at me.

"Okay, okay, okay." I knitted my fingers and sat up straighter in my chair. "At first it was really weird because she didn't acknowledge me at all. Like, she shook my hand but not in any way different from everyone else. I actually started to think she didn't remember…you know…"

"Your winter fling?"

"Exactly."

She scrunched up her face. "Well, you said 'at first'. What happened in the second act?"

I scoffed. "Soccer doesn't have acts, remember? We've been over this. It's different from theatre."

"You and I both know it's completely the same. Now, what happened?"

"Sure. Anyway, then, after the game it was weird because she shook my hand, you know, like normal, but then…"

Her eyes widened and she shifted forward in her seat. "Yeah?"

"She didn't let go. She, like, held on and put her hand on my shoulder."

She leaned forward so much I worried she might topple off. "And then?"

"Then, she stroked my shirt with her thumb. And said my name." I grimaced. It sounded so lame.

But, as usual, Viv's reaction didn't fail to disappoint. She gasped long and loud and brought her hand to her throat. If she'd been wearing pearls she would have clutched them.

"Quick," she said. "Role-play it with me."

"Ew, what? No. I don't see why you're freaking out. Don't you think she's bad to the bone?"

She shrugged. "Who cares what I think? I know what she means to you. I might be the only one who knows. It's actually nice to see you fired up about someone. When you talk about all the other girls you date you're so blasé."

"Like the cherries?"

She snorted. "That's glacé. I mean, you never seem to care that much about them. Out of sight, out of mind. Now role-play this handshake with me! I want to picture it. If you don't, I'll play the *Waitress* soundtrack outside your bedroom door so you can't sleep."

I groaned but stood up from my comfy chair. "You'll have Coach to answer to. Minimum nine hours' sleep during the tournament."

"Yeah, yeah, yeah. Now, I'm you and you're Christine. We shake hands…yep, good. Now I go to end the shake and you…"

I held on gently and put my hand on Viv's shoulder and ran my thumb along the hollow under her collarbone.

She yelped. "Holy shit! Is that what she did to you? Engaged in literal foreplay in front of millions of worldwide viewers. I need a cold shower and a lie-down. But she said something to you?"

"Just my name."

"How? How did she deliver it?"

I scrunched up my face. "Uhhhh, I dunno. Like…" I stared into Viv's eyes, still clasping her hand, my other hand on her shoulder. "Keeley."

"Okay, okay. We can workshop that. Your accent is way off. Was it like this?" She adjusted her shoulders and lifted her chin. "Keeley."

I grimaced. "What was *that*? Your Robert DeNiro impression?"

"Shut up! Isn't she from Brooklyn?"

"No, you sausage. That was Kelly Deveraux. Christine's from Tacoma."

"Ohhh, right. Okay, here goes…Keeley."

I screwed up my nose. Not quite right. "Keeley."

"Keeley." Viv's voice was barely above a sultry whisper.

"Nuh, nuh, nuh. Keeley."

"Keeeeeeley."

"What are you doing?" asked Fletch.

We wheeled around, our hands flying off each other.

"Just re-enacting Keeley's reunion with—Ow!"

I had crashed up next to her and grabbed her arm, accidentally treading on her toes. "With Amber Hatfield."

"That popstar? I didn't know you'd met up with her again."

"No, um, I mean, if I ever, well, reunite with her. I need to practice what I'd do. Viv was helping me role-play."

"Oh." Fletch pressed their lips together and glanced at the fire. "You've never seemed nervous about talking to women."

"You're so right, Fletch," Viv said. "Keeley is usually the picture of nonchalance, because she doesn't really care how it ends up, one way or another. But she seems to have stumbled across someone who makes all that easy confidence fly out the window."

My chest tightened a little. I opened my mouth to speak, but nothing came out. *Shitballs.* Maybe she was right.

Fletch looked from me to Viv a few times. "I see. Well, I forgot my phone out here." They picked it up off the arm of one of the chairs. "I'll see you in the morning."

After the door had shut behind them Viv slapped me across the arm. "Way to mangle my toes, Stompy. I've got rehearsals for the *Guys and Dolls* chorus tomorrow." She sat down and rubbed her foot through her purple Ugg boot.

I crouched down next to her chair and put both my hands on her forearm. "Sorry. I don't want the team to know about me and Christine, that's all."

"Okay, 'the team' is one thing, but what about Fletch? Lying to them—" She held her finger up to stop me interrupting. "Even lying by omission, is like lying to the sweetest, most good creature on the planet."

"Most good?"

She ignored me. "It's like lying to…to, Pikachu! You're lying to Pikachu. If, you know, Pikachu were tall, dark and good-looking."

"Pikachu is capable of vicious attacks involving a dangerous amount of electricity."

She rolled her eyes.

"All right. Look, you know keeping secrets stresses Fletch out. Remember they got that rash when they couldn't tell their Nanna about her surprise birthday party?"

She slumped back in her chair. "I'd forgotten about that. But I still don't get why you're keeping Christine a secret at all. No one will care."

"I know, I know. It's just…When I first made the national team, I was so worried about blowing it that I kept everything low-key. You know? No drama, no intrigue—just soccer."

"Yeah, but now you're part of the furniture. Your love life literally made the front page of the newspaper when you jumped on that big bin, and they didn't drop you."

"They didn't drop me, but Coach said she didn't want my personal life to cause any more distractions. My history with Christine is just that—a distraction."

"History?" She raised her eyebrows at me.

I leaned my chin on my hands. Unexpectedly, tears start to well up.

Viv had been right—I did care about Christine. But it was stupid. She had stone cold dropped me years ago.

"Well, no chance of anything but history," I said. My voice caught a little. "It's not like I'll bump into her down at the corner store anytime soon. Plus, you're forgetting a major factor here—she has a girlfriend."

Viv frowned, her big eyes also welling up in sympathy. "Ohhhhh, crap. That Cora woman. I forgot about that little detail. But you do still have feelings for her?"

I shrugged. "If I did they'd be about as much use as a chocolate teapot. I'd better get to bed."

I stood, feeling exhausted.

Viv took my hand. "Hey, make sure you don't wish your emotions away. You've been on auto-pilot too long. You might learn something about yourself through this struggle."

I kissed her on the top of the head. "You're psychic, you little weirdo. I was just wishing the middle of my chest had a big off switch."

She wrapped her arms around my middle. "Good night."

"Good night. And if I adapt this sadness into an experimental one-woman show, I'll comp you a ticket."

My eyes were red in the mirror as I brushed my teeth. *Feelings.* That's what I'd told Viv I had for Christine. But what feelings? My insides were a whirl. Attraction, doubt, joy, and, yes, pain when I thought about her leaving three years ago.

I sighed. It was important I got a good night's sleep. Where was my giant off switch when I needed it?

Chapter 11

We won our next match against Denmark five goals to one. Because of the loss to the US, we would need to win our remaining group stage match to make the finals.

That afternoon's Denmark match had been in the beautiful new stadium near the river in Perth, built a few years ago. I had played well, and Coach had mentioned me in the post-match rundown as being an on-field leader for discipline and sticking to our gameplan.

A few hours after dinner in the hotel dining room, Fletch and I were lying on twin beds with the lights off. Fletch flicked channels on the big TV.

"Ooh, *Private Benjamin*! I love this movie. Happy with this?"

"Uh-huh," I replied, not looking up from my phone. I was scrolling hard through Christine's Instagram again. The account had started right when she got her big deal with Reebok, four months after she'd dropped out of Florida State and out of my life.

I chucked my phone down. I was sick of thinking about her. Maybe I needed to see some sort of counsellor about this unhealthy obsession that had spread like wildfire since our on-field moment the week before. Christine had to be the most unavailable woman to me on the entire planet—she was a superstar who lived on the other side of the world, not to mention she was in a de facto relationship with a bikini model/snowboarder/appeared on an episode of *Real Housewives of Salt Lake City* one time because her aunt was married to an upholstery mogul. I was pretty free and easy in my relations with the girls of the world, sure, but I never ever messed with people who had partners.

I sighed and lay back to stare at the ceiling. The TV was blaring an ad for an electronics chain called Altronics.

"They've got weirdo shops over here in the west," I said to the empty air above my bed.

"It's so different over here. Did you know Perth is the most remote state capital in the world? Surrounded by practically nothing but sea and desert," Fletch said.

"Who died and made you Google?"

"Hah! You're a dag."

I rolled on my side to look at them. In the insane washed out blue and grey light of the TV they looked like a little kid.

"I don't get how you can watch ads," I said.

"I like them. The internet connection was always a bit iffy when I was growing up, so free-to-air telly was all we had. My brothers and sisters and I could recite them all, and sing along to all the music."

I suddenly couldn't speak. The thought of little Fletch and all their siblings singing along merrily to a floor coverings superstore jingle, for some reason, made me choke up. This crazy adventure we were on took us a long way from home. I loved my team and I loved the game we played, but sometimes I felt tired of the constant pressure, striving and discipline. And hotel beds, lobbies, airports and continental breakfasts in huge freezing hotel dining rooms. It's like that Paul Kelly song—after a while *Every Fucking City Looks the Same.*

I rolled off the bed and slammed my feet down on the cheap carpet. "I'm going to get some air," I said, scrambling for my sneakers and pulling them on.

"But, it's late," Fletch said, pulling their attention from Goldie Hawn with some effort.

"Yeah, well, we're not under house arrest, are we?" I grabbed a key card out of the little paper sleeve thing they gave us at the front desk, pulled my jacket on and pushed the door open. "I won't be long."

"Okay—" They didn't sound like they thought it was one hundred per cent okay, but the door closed heavily behind me and I strode down the hallway.

It was quiet outside on the street. Perth wasn't known for its wild and crazy nightlife. I stood for a second. I knew the city a bit from my years of coming over when Melbourne Victory played Perth Glory in the national league.

"Downhill leads to the water," I said under my breath. I turned to my left and let the gravity of the slight descent of the footpath lead me, hopefully, to the open air of the big, wide Swan River.

I walked a few blocks and the air got fresher and cooler, so I knew I was headed in the right direction. Sure enough, a little way ahead I was able to cross the street diagonally to a strip of grass criss-crossed with bike paths, and then, reaching the welcome still, open space of the river, I almost ran across the grass to the low metal fence on the bank. I took a deep breath and hugged my chest as I exhaled long and loud. My shoulders loosened and dropped. I hadn't realised I'd been tensing them up so tight.

There were a handful of people around still, couples walking home from the pub maybe.

To my left a few hundred metres away a large yacht was moored—music and voices reached me when the air was still, but were carried off when the sea breeze gusted.

The Swan River was so wide the lights on the opposite bank were tiny orbs and it was impossible to make out what they were. I emptied my mind and let my eyes drift to the inky blackness to my right that was the Indian Ocean, then back to the cliffs on my side of the river. At the very top, some of the trees in Kings Park were illuminated.

Maybe every city didn't look the same, especially this big flat oasis in the middle of the desert. And maybe I was going to be okay. I could just stop obsessing over Christine, just think about soccer and my friends and my family. Surely happiness lay at the end of that path. I could right now be hanging out by this river, thinking about how I'd played a great game of soccer for my country that day.

I grabbed onto the railing and leaned back to look at the stars. I would take up meditation.

A memory surfaced of Christine teaching me how to meditate the night before we got together. No train of thought was safe!

I was driving myself crazy trying to find answers to impossible questions. Why couldn't I shake this dumb college fling from years ago? Why did a single moment of attention from Christine light a spark that made me feel like I'd been asleep for years and had suddenly been jolted awake? Was I broken somehow?

"*Gah!* Who gives a shit anyway?" I said, putting my chin to my chest and squeezing my eyes tight shut.

I hit my palms against the railing in front of me and exhaled. I breathed in deeply through my nose. The roiling whirlpool of thoughts in my head started to dissipate. I hugged my middle. It was time to go back to Fletch and get some sleep.

I was reluctant to leave the big expanse of water that had brought me some comfort, and I figured I could walk along the bank toward the cliffs for a bit then cut back to the hotel through the city streets from there.

I threw my head back as I started walking, relishing the simple movement of my body and the sense of freedom it brought. The wind dropped and the night became still and quiet. The river looked like a black mirror.

Movement caught my eye up ahead on the path. I scoffed and shook my head. *Perfect.* I had gone for a walk to get Christine out of my head and now a woman who looked exactly like her was walking toward me.

I kept on walking.

The woman looked out at the river, then caught sight of me and slowed. *Shit, that really does look like her.* I didn't slow down. The sooner I got close enough for my brain to realise my eyes were playing tricks on me, the better.

The woman slowed even more—now she was barely putting one foot in front of the other and her eyes were fixed on me.

Holy fucking hellballs. It *was* Christine. I had a mad urge to run sideways and hide behind a big gum tree. I slowed right down too so, like two dead stars locked in each other's gravity, we moved through no will of our own.

We came to a stop facing each other. I could still feel the gravitational pull, but I planted my feet to the ground. She was dressed almost identically to me, sweats with her jacket collar pulled up against the night chill.

I could see her breath as she exhaled. My gaze rested on her lips and I was hit with the memory of the way her mouth felt against mine. A shock ran up the back of my neck. What the hell was I doing? Fixating on stuff that had happened years ago like an obsessed stalker.

I cleared my throat. She looked tense as hell, standing with her arms locked by her sides. Did she have some idea of what was going on in my head?

"Hey," she said, then immediately pressed her lips together.

I could feel my eyes screwing up. This was intensely awkward.

"What are you doing here?" I asked, but Christine had spoken at the same time and I'd missed what she'd said.

"What?" we both said in unison.

She smiled. My stomach dropped so fast I thought my knees might give way. She really was incredibly beautiful.

"I owe you an apology," she repeated.

"Huh?"

"I've been turning it over in my mind. It's been bothering me actually. I, uh…" She shook her head and smiled again. *Hell, I'm going to drop dead!* "When I saw you, I had the insane thought that maybe I'd willed you here by wanting to talk to you. Isn't that the most self-centred thing you've ever heard?"

The breeze picked up out of nowhere and all the gum trees lining the river swooshed and started to sway. There was not another soul around. A profound feeling of unreality settled on me. I put my hand into my pocket and pinched my leg hard. Nope, I wasn't dreaming. And I would have a bruise tomorrow.

I wanted to reach over and touch her. I squeezed my hands into fists. The weird surrealness intensified. There was a brief time in this world where it would have been natural for me to brush my fingers down her cheek. She used to move sideways and catch the tip of my thumb with her lips. I shoved my balled hands further into my pockets.

Time was a construct, wasn't it? No, wait, it's relative. I had borrowed Fletch's copy of *A Brief History of Time* but hadn't gotten through the first ten pages. I knew one thing though—the consequences of straight-up tongue-kissing someone else's girlfriend were neither relative nor a construct.

Oh brother! Christine raised her eyebrows. Had she asked me a question? I was starting to sweat despite the cold. She was going to think I was on hard drugs, and not the performance enhancing kind.

"Will you walk with me?" she asked.

I nodded. *Get me out of this deserted, unreal time slip!* I hoped she would take me somewhere bustling with people who might recognise us and would hold me accountable for anything I said or did.

"We're at the Ritz-Carlton," she said, setting off the way she'd come.

"Ooh, swisho," I said, falling into step beside her. Of course the US team had booked out the fanciest and most expensive hotel in town. We were at a glorified Holiday Inn. I relaxed my fingers from their death-grip. It was a relief to form a thought that wasn't connected to how much I wanted to throw myself at Christine.

She laughed. A loud *ha!* that was unexpected and real. She looked sideways at me, still smiling. I shouldn't have looked at her but I couldn't tear my eyes away. I squeezed my fists up so tight I risked causing permanent damage to the circulation in my fingers.

"I remember you always used to say funny, random things," she said.

My ears started to burn. What else did she remember?

"I felt like I needed to apologise for rushing off so quickly after the game last week. It would have been nice to catch up more, after all this time. But I got dragged off for an interview..."

My mouth felt very dry all of a sudden. "It's fine," I managed to say. But it didn't feel fine. I wasn't expecting her to bring up how she'd looked at me, how she'd touched me after the last match. But here we were, talking about it. Viv always told me I had a terrible poker face. Did Christine have a clue about the feelings she'd stirred up inside me, under the lights, surrounded by cameras?

"Oh good. It's fine," she said. The words sounded strange—very flat.

I kept my head down and my eyes straight ahead. My eyes burned. I very much wanted to be back in my narrow bed listening to Fletch's gentle snores.

"I like getting out by myself before big games. It helps me clear my head," she said.

"I remember." I said the words without thinking. The last thing I wanted to do was take the conversation back to years before—to acknowledge what we'd been to each other.

Still I kept my eyes fixed straight ahead. She was silent beside me.

Then she cleared her throat. "I've been craving more and more alone time recently. More walks." A pause. "How about you?"

I turned the question over in my mind. *Am I going on more walks now than usual? What have I been craving?* I gave up. "What do you mean?" I asked.

"Oh, uh, are you alone much?"

I scrunched up my forehead. This conversation was a confusing wild ride! "Just the normal amount, I suppose. My housemates are always around, but they're great so I don't mind."

I glanced over, wondering what on earth she was going to say next. She didn't meet my eyes.

We reached the street and, thankfully, there were a few other people hurrying by under the streetlights.

I saw the illuminated sign for Christine's hotel ahead. *Thank heavens!* A couple stood next to a mountain of luggage on the footpath. One of their suitcases was flat on the ground and a small child was curled up fast asleep on top of it clutching a soft toy that looked like a blue cattle dog. Christine kept walking right past the door.

"Hey, aren't you staying here?" I whispered. I didn't want to wake the kid.

"Yeah, the hotel's got the team using the side entrance. You know how those well-meaning supporters wanting selfies can clog up a foyer. It's this way."

We made it to the street corner and she made a left. Ahead of us alongside the hotel was a car park with two big Greyhound-style buses in it. She climbed easily over a chain slung low across driveway entrance.

I climbed over too, almost catching my foot. I pulled off a couple of big hops, my arms flailing, to keep from falling over.

Our footsteps were loud as we crossed the car park, lit by aggressive security lights on tall poles. A car went by along the street behind us. I wondered out of nowhere if it was the sleeping kid's Uber. *Uh-oh.* My brain was disassociating from how awkward this silent stroll with Christine was becoming.

"The door's just through here. Do you have a minute?"

Ahead of us was a barely lit path through some nice gardens the hotel obviously tended to very well. Even at night it looked welcoming and secluded and pleasant. There wasn't a snowball's chance in hell I was walking into that oasis with her.

She slowed to a halt when I didn't reply. I stopped too, but kept looking ahead, my shoulders awkwardly at right angles to her.

She took a step toward the path but I didn't follow. A part of me wanted to bound after her, but a bigger part reared back like a horse that sensed danger in the equestrian portion of the modern pentathlon. Christine wheeled around.

"I can't," I said. "Look, I don't want to make this weird, well, weirder than it is already, but...I'm going to go." I started to turn, then stopped and winced. I didn't want Christine to think I was pissed off, but I had to get out of there. "See ya," I said, then flinched. That sounded even angrier.

"Wait." She took half a step toward me then stopped short, dropping her hands to her sides. "Look, um, you don't owe me anything. At all. I just...don't like the feeling that you're going to be completely gone from my life again." She grabbed her phone out of her pocket and thrust it toward me. "Will you give me your number. Please?"

I stood, frozen. *I should say no.* But something had clicked in me when she said she didn't want me to disappear. I got it. Because deep down I didn't want her to be lost to me either.

I took her phone and tapped in my number. She put it away again quickly, like she was hiding it.

I'd had more confusion than I could handle for one evening. I needed to get out of there. "Good night," I said. This time I managed to walk away.

"Bye," she said.

I didn't turn around. I couldn't risk it.

Chapter 12

Fletch was asleep when I got back to our room. I tiptoed around getting ready for bed then lay there, tense as a board, eyes wide open.

What. The. Hell. Had that whole encounter been a mad hallucination? Had I tumbled over the bank of the Swan River and hit my head?

We didn't touch, we didn't talk about the past. But there had been a seismic energy shift.

Get a grip! Nothing had happened. Christine had, what, asked me what percentage of my day I spent alone? Told me she had willed me to a deserted bike path with the power of her mind?

Maybe the big takeaway here was that the pressures of being a top-flight athlete had made her a bit strange.

There was something there though. She had been tense as hell when we'd run into each other. Not unusual for someone seeing an ex unexpectedly. But if that's all there was to it, why ask me to walk with her, and why ask for my number?

I rubbed my eyes with the heels of my hands. I had a massive day of physical recovery and match review in a few short hours. There was no point going round in circles about Christine. Even if she had felt a tiny fraction of the fizz I got when I'd made her laugh tonight, it didn't matter. She wasn't good at being in relationships.

I remembered hearing that from the person closest to her in the whole world.

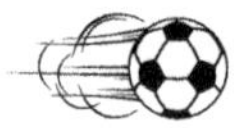

A few weeks after we'd gotten together after the last game of the college season, we had met her sister at a Chinese restaurant within walking distance of campus. Lori was a flight attendant and had been on a one-night stopover in Tallahassee.

I had felt ten feet tall walking along under the streetlights with Christine's hand in mine. She caught my eye and smiled, grabbing onto my arm with her other hand and rubbing my elbow through my jacket.

She looked amazing. In soccer season she only ever wore her hair regimentally straightened and pulled back into a pony, but since we'd won the big game she's been letting it get a little loose, and tonight had it pulled back into two puffy buns at the base of her neck. Under her warm jacket she wore a green patterned loose-fitting jumpsuit that was tight at the waist and clung in all the right places to show off her amazing hips and legs.

"Are you sure it's okay I'm taking up your sister's whole visit? I can meet you guys after for a drink if you want to catch up properly."

"No, don't be silly. She's always kind of zombie-like on these one-night stopovers. I'm going to visit her for Christmas break in, like, a couple of weeks anyway. I want you here. Plus, she's dying to meet you."

My biggest smile didn't feel big enough. "You two are close, yeah?"

She nodded. "Lori was my whole world for a lot of my childhood. She's seven years older and, well, when my mom wasn't around much, then she eventually left, Lori practically raised me. Dad worked, like, all the time, so it was often just her and me."

Her grip on my arm loosened a little but she didn't let go.

I squeezed her hand but didn't speak. Christine had given me little glimpses of her life before FSU in the time we'd spent together, but they'd been few and far between. I'd never wanted to push her for information. There was no rush. However, if she was in the mood to talk, I was more than happy to listen.

"Lori always denied it, but I've always thought the three of them—Lori, Mom and Dad—were a happy, balanced little family before I came along. Manageable and simple. My mom…she's not able to handle much. She could never get the drive and energy behind anything long enough to make it work. Including being a parent, I guess."

"Oh, I'm so sorry. That must have been really hard."

"Yeah. I was kind of a crappy kid, you know. Stubborn. I remember just being so unhappy all the time. It was better after mom and dad finally got divorced and it was mainly just me and Lori."

We reached the restaurant and I cast around for something to say. I wanted to put both my arms around her. But just then a woman with a dark mass of corkscrew curls jumped up from a table and waved at us with both hands through the window.

Christine gasped and waved back. "There she is! Come on." She pulled me by the hand through the door.

"Come here, my baby," said Lori, pulling Christine into a massive hug. "And you, Keeley!" She hugged me too, then gave me a kiss on both cheeks. "Look at the pair of you! The best-looking couple I've seen in a long while—and Shawn Mendes and Camilla Cabello were on my flight last week!"

"Nice to meet you, Lori. You're, uh, a really good hugger."

"Would you *listen* to that Aussie accent. To *die* for!" she said, looking sideways at Christine.

I stood there and grinned, wondering what to say next. Lori was not what I expected. I had thought she'd be like a seven-years-older Christine—serious and precise, her flight attendant uniform pressed and pristine. This woman was downright bubbly. She wore purple leopard-print leggings and a T-shirt that had the word 'princess' and a picture of a crown in shiny gold.

"Sit, sit, sit. Let's order. Do you eat normal food, Keeley, or just steamed broccoli and poached chicken like Teenie's last girlfriend at Northwest? Boy, did she smell bad!"

Teenie! I didn't even mind the mention of an ex. The childhood nickname was too adorable.

"Lori! Stop."

"Don't stop," I said, resting my chin on my hand and plastering on my best listening face.

Lori laughed and slapped me on the arm. “Oh, the stories I could tell you. But let’s order first. I haven’t eaten since I had a tuna salad sandwich over Wichita.”

I really started to enjoy myself. Lori was like a glowing ball of warm energy. Christine’s face when she looked at her was so full of affection that it made my tummy do little flips. She looked even more beautiful when she was radiating love for her big sister.

During the meal Lori had us in stitches with a story of a woman who had threatened to storm into the cockpit unless the captain agreed to stop a barking dog she could hear from the luggage bay.

“She was all like ‘My turtle Trudy is down there too! She gets stressed out by loud noises and her Valium only lasts another forty minutes! Trudy, *TRUDY!*’ We had to radio ahead to get the Marshall to handle her after we landed. Giving a turtle Valium. Can you even? They’re already so slow!”

After the meal was done Christine stood up to visit the bathroom. When she was out of sight Lori came to sit next to me.

“Is she treating you right, honey?”

I gaped like a goldfish then clamped my mouth shut. “Aren’t you meant to ask if *I’m* treating *her* right?”

She threw her head back and laughed. “I like you. You’re not going to just take any old bullshit. No, see, I love my baby sister, but she always runs in the opposite direction of the people that can do her good. When she cares, she pushes away. Me, I held her tight even though she tried to push me away from when she was five, right up to when she was fifteen.”

I laid both my hands palm down on the table. “I really like her. And she’s been great to me since we got together. It hasn’t been long, but she’s been great every day.”

Lori took both my hands in hers. “It makes me feel so good to hear that.” She dropped her voice low and leaned in. “She really likes you. She’s been telling me about you on the phone for months.”

“Really?”

“For months and months! ‘Keeley kicks the ball to me nice. Keeley thought biscuits were cookies and got a surprise when she ordered them with coffee at a diner in Fort Worth, Keeley says Britney Spears hasn't released a good album since 2004.'"

"I never said that! *Blackout* is a masterpiece."

"When she phoned me saying she'd made a move and you liked her back, I screamed and scared a whole lot of people waiting to check in at Chicago O'Hare. People are so jumpy in airports."

I leaned back in my chair. There was a glow in my chest at what Lori was telling me, but then a little twinge of disappointment that Christine hadn't told me all this herself. I told myself I was being silly—we'd only been dating a few weeks after all.

Christine appeared at the back of the restaurant.

Lori squeezed my hands then whispered as she stood up. "She better not fuck this up for the two of you."

"Again, shouldn't you be telling *me* not to fuck it up?"

She laughed again. "I've got a good feeling about you, Keeley McGee."

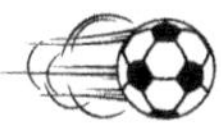

Any good feelings I had about myself and Christine as a couple came crashing down not long after. It was the second-last day before winter break, but our professors were working us right up until the last minute. Cruelly, Florida State held most of its final exams right after the break, so I was going to have to study at least a little bit while I was home for Christmas.

As usual, my mind strayed to Christine. She would be madly studying too. Her last class was the following afternoon, then she was heading back to Tacoma.

I wondered what she would tell the rest of her family about me. I was going to tell everyone—mum, dad, aunts, cousins, second cousins, even my three-year-old third cousin, Zane. He had the right to know, surely? I was going to bore everyone to death at Christmas lunch describing how pretty and cool and good at soccer Christine was.

I checked my phone. 4:45 p.m. I groaned. It was later than I thought and I still had so much to do. I had a flight from Orlando booked for the following evening to fly to Brisbane. I would have to put in a few solid hours before I could go out for dinner with Christine tonight.

She'd made us a reservation at a little Mexican place downtown for our last date before break. I smiled to myself.

I opened my computer again but threw my head back in defeat immediately. My eyes burned, my neck was stiff, and I had the beginnings of a headache in my left frontal lobe.

I jumped up and grabbed a handful of coins from my desk drawer. I would head down to the only vending machine on campus that had passionfruit Fanta. The sugar content was so high it made my pupils dilate and my heart pump uncomfortably. It was exactly what I needed. Plus, the walk might realign my spine.

Pulling up the hood of my sweater, I walked out into the cool grey evening and plunged my hands into my pockets. The air was crisp against my face as I walked past one dorm building and another toward my goal.

I rounded a corner and nearly ran headlong into someone. I dodged, catching a glimpse of long blonde hair.

"Oh, sorry," I said as I went to continue on.

"Keeley."

I stopped. "Oh, hey, Bethany."

I had met Christine's roommate briefly as she headed out the door one evening at the same time I was arriving, Cheetos in hand, to watch a movie with Christine. She had been giving Christine and me a lot of space the last couple of weeks. Christine said Bethany didn't mind, but I still appreciated it.

To my surprise Bethany frowned and put her hand on my shoulder. "How are you holding up, babe, now the good-bye is getting so close? She told me this morning and I actually cried."

My mind tried to make what she had said make sense. *Nope!* Couldn't do it. "Sorry, who told you what?"

"Christine. How she's not coming back next semester."

"What?"

Her mouth fell open and she opened her eyes wide. "Oh no, oh no, oh no! I thought for sure she would have told you. She must have some reason, babe. Look, I've gotta run. Sorry, uh, bye!"

She grabbed my shoulders and gave me a quick kiss on the cheek, then stood for a second and shook her head as if she didn't quite know why she'd done it, then practically ran out of sight.

My feet were rooted to the spot. Surely Bethany had it wrong. Christine wouldn't be dropping out of Florida State the next day and not have told me. Bethany was studying chemistry and didn't seem like a dummy, but sometimes those science types had their heads in the clouds. Christine had probably just been telling her about her trip home. She must have been confused as hell when Bethany burst into tears!

I reached for my phone but realised I didn't have it. I looked around. I was one building away from Christine's dorm. I knew Bethany must have the wrong end of the stick, but I broke into a jog anyway.

I tapped on Christine's door. I was hot in the hallway in my hoodie and my heartrate was up. I tried the door handle and the door swung open. Christine was crouched on the floor next to a big open suitcase, earbuds in, balling up a pair of socks. She looked up as the door opened. She jumped to her feet and clenched her jaw, standing stock still. I registered that was a weird reaction to seeing me, at the same time I registered that her desk and shelves were bare, and her Abby Wambach and Simone Biles posters were gone.

That's odd. I closed the door behind me. "Whatcha doing?"

She took her buds out and placed them on the bed behind her.

Maybe she hadn't heard me.

"What's going on? Are you changing rooms?"

She intertwined her fingers in front of her chest. It was a weird motion, almost like she was protecting herself. "No, not quite. I'm leaving."

"Yeah, to go to Tacoma for break."

"No. As in, yes, I'm doing that, but I'm not coming back after. Seattle Reign FC have offered me a contract. Guaranteed starting first eleven in the Challenge Cup in March, then the national women's soccer league in August. I'm going to finish my degree at Washington State."

My head felt as if it was full of thick porridge. I couldn't make the wheels turn. I squinted.

She took a step toward me. "It's the best women's soccer league in the world, a fast-track to national team selection. They hardly ever sign college students before we've finished the NCAA cycle. It's really, really rare." She frowned and bit her bottom lip.

A weight started to press down on my chest. "When were you going to tell me?"

"Tonight at dinner."

I closed my eyes. Numb shock started to give way to a burning in my throat.

"A crowded public place. Nice. So I wouldn't make a scene."

"Keeley, no. It's not like that—"

"I'm surprised you didn't put the news in a Christmas card and send it Air Mail to me when I was on the other side of the world."

"Hey, no, that's hardly fair. I thought it would be better this way. That you would be happy for me."

My face seared. "When did you know?" I asked her, my voice low and cold.

Her hands fell to her sides. Her eyes slid away from mine and down to the floor. "Ten days ago. I got the confirmation call and signed the contract ten days ago."

I closed my eyes. I wanted to crumple to the floor. But I didn't. I planted my feet and looked across at her, this girl I liked so goddamned much, more than anyone else, ever. She had been so tender, sweet—hell, even loving since we'd hooked up. But right then, as she bit her bottom lip and picked at her thumbnail, she may as well have been a stranger.

"So, what was this? Did you just want to have 'the girlfriend experience' for a bit of fun while you busily planned your new life in Seattle?"

"No, no way. That's not how it was, how it is, at all."

"Then what? I'm racking my brains, Christine. Because, you know, I thought I knew what was going on, and now I feel like a fucking moron."

She put her arm across her chest, gripping her elbow with her opposite hand. "We were having so much fun. I didn't want to ruin it. I thought we could make the most of the time I had left here. I mean, I can see I've got it wrong, but I didn't do any of this to hurt you."

I scoffed. White hot fury coursed through my limbs. "Fun? *Fun?*" I looked at the ceiling then nodded. "You know what, I was right about you at the start. You don't feel things properly like normal people. I don't know why you decided to play me. But I know for sure this sucks, and you suck, and I never want to speak to you again."

Her mouth dropped open, and she took a step toward me, but I spun away from her and opened the door, fumbling slightly. I closed it behind me and ran down the hall without looking back.

The next day, I sunk further down in the plastic, bucket-like seat and hugged my big backpack with both arms. Viv had come with me on the bus to Orlando Airport. I was glad of the company—although she kept looking at me side-long like I might start wailing and gnashing my teeth.

It had been twenty-four hours since my visit to Christine's dorm.

"Another Dunkin'?" she asked brightly, offering me the box.

"Yes, please," I said, taking a custard-filled donut. "Sorry. I'm not much fun to be around."

My insides felt grey and heavy. I had been looking forward to this trip home, but when I tried to think ahead to seeing everyone I had been missing, I couldn't conjure a single spark of happiness. I sighed.

Viv rubbed my arm then gave it a little pat. "You've done the right thing, you know."

"I think I know. It's just like, I'm gaslighting myself or something. What if what she did wasn't so bad? Like she said, the last ten days wouldn't have been as amazing if I'd known she was leaving."

Viv put her hands on my knees and swung around like a little ninja so she was crouching down in front of me. "No, Keeley. No." She slapped my knees with her palms as she said it.

I winced.

"She strung you along. She was talking out both sides of her mouth the whole time. It's actually psychotic, to not tell you what was going on, then pull the rug out from under you at the last minute.

You don't want someone like that in your life. You've dodged a bullet, especially since…" She raised her shoulders and looked very awkward.

"It's all right. Yes, especially since I was acting like she was the best thing since sliced bread."

"Yes, very that."

I ate more of my donut. "She was just so cool and awesome, you know? Being with her I felt ten feet tall."

"You're way too good for her. I know it stings that every kiss was real for you but a lie for her. But it just means you're capable of love. You're going to live a happy and full life. She's going to, like, use her soccer fame to start a crazy pyramid scheme. Or a cult!" Her eyes got a faraway look and I knew she was following the dramatic story she'd just come up with to its climactic conclusion, probably imagining playing herself in the made-for-tv adaptation of the story. "I knew something wasn't right from the beginning," she mumbled.

The boarding call went out to first class passengers and frequent flyers.

I dragged my phone out of the front pocket of my bag and tapped the screen. Two new messages—some teammates wishing me a safe trip. I hung my head a little.

Viv leaned against me, resting her head in the crook of my neck. Her blonde hair felt feathery and soft. "Promise me you'll try to enjoy your trip home, hey? She's not worth you ruining your Christmas over."

"Yeah, mate. You're right," I replied.

My stomach gave a gentle jolt because I was telling a lie. Maybe I just didn't want to admit I'd been wrong about Christine. That's why people stay in cults so long, after all, throwing good money after bad.

But even though my brain had worked overtime to convince me she was a two-faced, cynical, manipulative liar, I had the feeling deep in my bones that she was special. She was really special to me, and I couldn't change that overnight. It didn't matter though. No calls, no texts, no apology. It was clear as day that I wasn't special to her. The weight in my chest got heavier.

I hugged Viv tighter and rested my chin on the top of her head. I took a deep breath and stilled my mind. I was sick to death of the constant loop that had been playing non-stop for nearly twenty-four hours. For a while I just sat and hugged my friend. There was nothing to decide, nothing to fight against, nothing that had to be achieved. I had been wrong about the girl I'd been sleeping with. She'd strung me along and I'd fallen for it, and now she wanted nothing more to do with me. My only job now was to exist, and to heal.

The boarding call for the plain old economy class people blasted over the loudspeakers.

I gave Viv a final squeeze. "This is me," I said, shifting and reaching for my backpack.

Viv jumped up and stood expectantly in front of me with her arms outstretched, as if we hadn't just been embracing for the last fifteen minutes solid at least. I smiled and gave her another big hug, lifting her up off the ground for a moment.

When I released her, she placed her hand flat on my heart. "Go. Heal. I'll be standing right here when you get back."

"Thanks, mate. We're going to have the best semester ever when I get back, just like we said." At that moment I couldn't imagine enjoyment. Fun. But I said the words anyway.

She smiled and held her hand to the side of my face. "The very best."

The line to board started moving. After one last hug and a kiss on the cheek, I joined its slow progress. Just before I descended the tunnel I gave Viv a wave. She was a fair distance away, so I'm sure she didn't notice that I also looked past her, scanning quickly. But nobody was racing into view, desperate to make things right before I boarded.

Christine was the fastest and most driven person I'd ever come across. If she had wanted to be here in time she would have been.

Chapter 13

2023

"Are you gonna eat that?" Fletch asked, eyeing off half a baked potato left on my plate.

"Nah, go for gold." I pushed the plate over to them.

"Sweet! Hey, are you all right mate? You were quiet watching the game. And it's fully weird for you not to finish your dinner."

I cursed Fletch's caring and attentive nature. I was still feeling weird from my run-in with Christine on the riverbank the night before. We'd watched the US win their match that afternoon on the telly at the hotel. A truly awful way to try and take my mind off Christine. She had played well and got a lot of the ball. It seemed as if the camera was never off her!

My phoned pinged in my pocket. I glanced down the long table at our captain, Allie. She wasn't looking my way. There was a rule against using phones during team dinner, but I slid mine out of my pocket, half-hid it in the tablecloth draping over my lap, and read the text from an unknown number.

Hi Keeley. I wanted to tell you that Cora and I are no longer together. From Christine.

Dropping my phone onto the carpet, I just sat, frozen. Why was Christine sharing this with me? Had she felt the need to explain the moment we'd shared after the full-time whistle the other night?

My mind whirled. I needed to be by myself for a minute. I reached down and scrabbled around on the floor until my fingers found my phone.

"I'm going for a walk," I told Fletch.

Their forehead creased. "But dessert's fruit salad. You love fruit salad."

"I'll see you later."

In the deserted hallway my phone pinged again.

Can you meet me?

I exhaled and leaned against the wall. The words floated around my head, but I couldn't string them together into a coherent thought. *Can. I. Meet. Her?*

Can I?

For years she had existed as a beautiful vision in my social media feed, often side by side with her impossibly photogenic girlfriend. But now she was in the same city as me, holding onto her phone, waiting for me to reply to her. Unattached and single.

A flicker of desire lit up inside me. I closed my eyes. The smart thing to do here would be to sprint down to Cottesloe Beach and throw my phone in the sea. Put Christine, our messy past, and the heavy emotions she stirred up, as far away from me as possible. Focus on the tournament—the games coming up that might be the most important of my life.

Yes, I would do the smart thing. I didn't owe her anything.

But there couldn't be any harm in telling her face to face.

Excellent! My smart head and the warm feeling in my blood finally agreed. We would meet Christine.

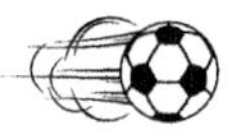

Perth's downtown was small and I walked the three blocks between her hotel and mine in no time. It felt later than it was. Like the night before, not many people were around.

She had asked that I meet her in the little carpark around the side of her hotel. I stepped over the low chain at the entrance and saw her. My breath caught in my throat. She was dressed almost exactly the same as the night before, but something was very different.

I gulped as I realised what it was. She wasn't someone else's girlfriend. And she had wanted me to know it.

All the resolutions my smart head had made were drowned out by a rushing in my ears.

"Hey," she said as I walked up to her.

"Hi."

"Thanks for coming."

I didn't reply.

She pressed her lips together and glanced up to the heavens. She looked just about as awkward as I felt.

She laced her fingers together and breathed out. "I, uh, I feel like I keep apologising to you. But I'm sorry. Again. It's insane for me to think you give a damn. But I wanted you to know about me and Cora."

"I was surprised. You two are, like, hashtag-couple-goals."

"Yeah, I, um, didn't want the news to break before the tournament. Bad news can be a distraction. And…" she laughed humourlessly. "Well, Cora has a partnership brand ambassadorship deal with Reebok in the works, and she didn't want to make any announcement until it was inked. And, yeah, I know how awful that sounds, but that's my life."

"Why—?" I began.

"A lot of reasons, I guess. Our public image and how much people loved us together used to be a fun sidenote to our relationship. But it became, you know, the most important thing. Cora started planning our dates based around which activities and places would look good on social media. I couldn't do it anymore."

"No, I meant, why did you tell me? About the breakup."

She glanced over my shoulder toward the street, relaxed her stance and exhaled. She stood not too close, but not too far away and her expression was almost uncannily neutral. Anyone looking at us would have thought we were discussing the recent rise in the price of some grocery items due to a confluence of factors including unpredictable weather and transport difficulties.

"I've thought about you a lot over the years, more and more recently as my relationship turned into a total cluster-fuck." She scoffed, her eyes not able to meet mine.

The ground was rushing up to meet me and there was no safety net.

She closed her eyes for a couple of seconds and took a deep breath. "I would think about how, you know, the time we spent together just felt…good. And fun. You know what I mean? I told myself that I just liked the person I was when I was with you, and of course, I dropped, rolled and bailed before things had a chance to get serious and, you get it, un-fun." She shifted her weight and glanced upwards. "But, seeing you at that game was like, goddamn, boom. Sparks fizzing about everywhere. I wasn't expecting it. Fireworks."

"They did have actual fireworks as we ran out, you know."

Her eyes locked onto mine, her face expressionless and intense. My brain had shaken off its shock and had caught up with current events. I wasn't frozen, or scared, or cringing with awkwardness anymore. I was so turned on I was almost uncomfortable. And in front of me was the insane, impossible possibility that I could have what I needed. I smiled slowly.

Christine narrowed her eyes and her lips parted. "Hmmmm. And was there a solo violin playing?"

"Cello, actually."

"You heard it too, hey?"

"I heard it too."

She took a step and leaned in. Her mouth was close to mine. I inhaled so hard it sounded like a strangled gasp. My entire body was charged with electricity.

"Follow me," she whispered. Her breath brushed against my cheek, sending waves of desire down my entire body.

She walked quickly off across the carpark. I ran to follow.

She stepped in between two of the big buses that sat parked and silent in the deserted carpark. There wasn't enough space for us to walk side by side, so I stopped to let her go ahead. It looked like she was walking down a very narrow corridor away from me, with the buses closing in on her on both sides like towering walls.

The lights illuminating the carpark didn't reach far into the narrow space, so I could barely make out her shape. I felt the loss of her as if a warm blanket had been ripped off me on a cold night. I ran again to catch up with her.

She stopped halfway down. My eyes started to adjust to the darkness. She stood with her back up against one of the buses. I stood across from her against the opposite bus. There was hardly any space between us at all.

She looked at me in silence. Then she swallowed hard. I watched her collarbone rise and fall as she breathed quickly. She raised her hand and touched two fingers to the hollow at her throat, as if she could feel my gaze on her skin.

I made a sound in the back of my throat that was half groan, half sigh. I lay my hands on her collarbone and felt the quick rise and fall of her breathing. She wrapped her arms around my waist and pulled me close to her. I pressed my face to hers, the bridge of my nose against her cheekbone.

Warmth shot through me and made my head spin. The feeling was one I'd never felt before, but it felt almost like relief. Intense, overwhelming relief. Like being home after a long absence. I released a shuddering breath.

Slowly, I lifted my lips to hers. Her tongue found mine gently and sent electricity right through me. The familiarity was glorious. My body remembered hers—her taste and smell, the little groan she gave ending in a gasp that was almost a squeak as I pressed her against the bus and kissed her harder.

She ran her hand down and pressed her fingers against my inner thigh. I groaned as all my awareness shot to just above her questioning hand.

She pulled back. Her lips were slick and swollen in the dimness. "Have I got this wrong?"

I smiled and kissed her earlobe, touching just the tip of my tongue to it. "Unless something very drastic has changed in the last few years," I whispered, "we both know you're never wrong."

I held her hip, my fingers questing under the waistband of her track pants and teasing the skin softly. She grabbed the back of my neck with both hands and kissed my mouth, her tongue finding mine. Then she pressed her lips to my neck.

"I've got the keys to the bus," she said. It came out a bit muffled and I wasn't sure I had heard right.

"Wait, what?"

Her voice was low and breathless. "This is the US women's national team bus. I have the keys."

"Huh?" I had a pleasant but urgent ache between my legs and all my brain could think of was taking Christine's clothes off and running my hands all over her body. "You want to drive somewh—wait, no, I'm an idiot."

She brought her lips close to mine. All my senses were filled up with her and I nearly swooned. "Whaddaya think?" she asked.

I bit my bottom lip. My body was on fire, but I hesitated. "I'm thinking…Fletch dropped a whole meat pie on their seat in our team bus the other day. There's still a brown stain. Is there any chance of a bed at all?"

Christine smiled and shook her head. "I wish there was, but I'm sharing a room." She wrapped her arms around my shoulders and put her forehead to mine. "I totally get it. It was a crazy idea. I want you, but it's enough for me that we've reconnected like this. It feels miraculous, actually. I'll let you get back to your hotel." Her arms started to loosen.

I gripped her waist tighter. "Nope!"

She kissed my mouth, laughing. "Nope? Well, I didn't want to sound pushy or desperate, but can I tell you it's a very clean bus? Like, spotless. Plus, our team nutritionist would never let us eat a meat pie. What even is that? The only things that should go in pies are apples or cherries. Or banana cream."

"Fine, fine! You win. Let's catch the bus."

She stepped sideways out of my grasp and clasped my hand, leading me to the heavily tinted glass door. Taking out a keyring with a few bits of black plastic strung onto it, she held them up to her face and fumbled around for the right one. Then she touched it to a panel next to the door and a red-lit digital keypad appeared. She keyed in some numbers and, after a pause, the door hissed then open inwards.

She took my hand again then started to climb the steps. I grabbed her around the waist with my free arm. Letting go of her hand I lifted her shirt and pressed my lips to the divot at the base of her spine.

"How is this bum even better than I remember?" I asked.

She turned and practically hauled me up into the bus by my armpits. "Get in here," she said, laughing. She gave the door a shove, then pressed a couple of buttons on the complicated keychain, huffing with impatience. "You need a fucking computer science degree to work this damn bus!" she said.

I spotted a small lever above the door and reached up as high as I could to pull it. The door hissed shut. I grinned in triumph. "Well, to be fair to the bus, you're probably meant to, you know, switch it on and drive it around. Not sneak in under the cover of darkness and..." I cocked my head to the side and narrowed my eyes.

We stood close together next to the driver's seat, a long aisle in front of us. With the door shut against the chilly night, it felt strangely like the rest of the world didn't exist anymore. The dark tinted windows only let the illumination of the carpark's floodlights in a little bit, and turned the interior a deep, velvet blue.

I took half a step closer to Christine so our bodies were touching. She inhaled sharply, then I felt her warm breath across my jaw.

I brushed my lips against hers. "There are fifteen hundred reasons we shouldn't do this," I said softly. I would have crumpled to the floor sobbing if she'd walked away from me in that moment, but I cared about her. In the very deepest fibre of my being I cared about her. We were both opening ourselves up to a lot of complications, drama and consequences we wouldn't like. I wanted her so badly that I didn't care about any of it, but she had always been so laser focused on her career.

"I know," she replied.

One big reason flashed through my mind. The memory of the cold look on her face when she told me she wasn't coming back to Florida State along with a flash of fear through my stomach. I looked at her now, holding on to me with desire written all over her face. Did I trust that she wouldn't devastate me again?

I kissed her, and she pressed herself against me. All my doubts melted away like a drug was kicking in. Besides, life didn't come with a written guarantee that I was never going to get hurt. I couldn't help wanting her, and I wasn't going to let fear get in my way.

She took my hand and guided it down, under the waistband of her sweats and undies. Her pussy was wet and slick. I moved my fingers, feeling her swell. I groaned. She gripped the hair at the back of my head with both hands so hard it made me lift my chin and gasp. It only intensified the wonderful pressure between my legs.

I gasped again and she brought her open mouth to mine, her tongue pressing against mine in time with the movements of my hand. Her breathing became a ragged pant at the back of her throat. She moved her hips against my fingers, guiding me deeper inside her. I wanted to, more than anything, but I also wanted to run my hands and mouth over her more completely. I stopped.

"Hey," I said breathlessly, "that backseat is looking mighty comfy."

"Good thinking." As I took my hand out of her pants, every atom of my being screamed "Nooooooo!" She grabbed my shoulders and jumped up to wrap her legs around my waist.

"I always loved how your muscles felt when you did this," she said, smiling down at me and running her hands over my shoulder blades and biceps. "Damn! You been lifting?"

I walked so fast down the aisle I hit my elbow on the raised armrest of one of the seats and winced.

"Yikes, are you okay?"

I plonked her down on the back seat. "I'm fine, except, I'm a bit worried. Could I die from being too turned on?"

She snorted. "Let's find out."

She ripped my jumper and shirt off and deftly undid my bra. I was still standing, and she knelt up on the seat and took my nipple in her mouth, licking it gently, while at the same time pulling my track pants and knickers down around my thighs. I unzipped her hoodie and pulled at her shirt. She helped me take it off, then pulled her white crop top up and over her head. We both grabbed a mishmash of our clothes and spread them out as best we could on the long back seat. I scrambled out of my pants, then laid Christine down. I kissed her below her belly button and slid off her sweats and underwear.

I paused for just a moment, running my eyes over the impossible beauty of her body, her soft breasts, the nipples already black and erect.

Then with an inelegant soft moan I ran my tongue up to her breasts and kissed and licked them eagerly, running my hands over her firm belly and down around her hips to hold onto her strong bottom. I felt her wetness rubbing against my belly. She shifted and ran her hand down and touched my clit. Pleasure shot through me. She dragged my face up toward her, again entwining her fingers at the back of my head and tugging me to where she wanted me.

"Hey, can we switch? Then I can use both hands," I said. I remembered she loved that.

"Oh, God. Yes please."

We had to slide past each other in the narrow space behind the seat in front and grinned as our bodies brushed together.

"It's not every night I'm nude on a bus with the enemy," I said. I grabbed whatever clothes were left and balled them into a makeshift pillow before lying down and shoving it under my head.

She scoffed as she straddled my hips, kneeling tall and staying upright.

"What?" I asked. "I want to be able to see without getting a neck strain! How would I explain that to the team physio?"

"Are you enjoying the show so far?" She took my hand and gently put my index and middle fingers in her mouth, dragging them slowly over her tongue and bottom lip.

In reply I ran both hands down from her neck, slowly across her breasts and belly, luxuriating in every centimetre of her skin. I touched my two wet fingers to her clit and she groaned and thrust against my hand. I moved my fingers back to her vagina and she closed her eyes tight, breathing "Yes!" and fumbling to grip the headrest of the seat next to her.

I went inside her with both fingers and gasped at the soft swollen wetness.

I moved in and out, getting deeper every time as she thrust and moved with me, her breathing becoming louder. Every breath became a loud exclamation that was halfway between a "yeah!" and an "ah!"

She became impossibly swollen and I brought the fingers of my other hand to her clit, pressuring and rubbing in time with her frantic movements.

She leaned over and gripped both sides of my ribcage, juddering and moaning as her vagina pulsed around my hands.

She shifted against me, moving down. She opened my legs wide, so one of my knees was jammed against the seat in front. Wordlessly she pressed her slick vagina against mine.

"Oh, God," I moaned.

She leaned down, her breasts moving against mine and her mouth close. "Does it feel good?" she asked.

"Uh-huh." I nodded then gasped as she thrusted again.

I started to lose all control. All my senses were full up. She kissed my mouth with swollen lips. I ran my hand up the back of her neck into her hair and held her fast, my tongue in her mouth. Her clit rubbed against mine with more urgency.

I moaned with no words. When I came I held her open mouth to mine as I gasped and juddered. She nuzzled her nose close to my ear, still moaning softly and breathing hard. She kept moving her wet pussy against mine. I ran both hands down her body and held onto her perfect arse, relishing the rhythmic movements it seemed like she had no control over.

She pressed her open mouth so hard against my cheekbone that I felt her teeth, and she let out a long ragged breath.

She rested her forehead to mine and slumped full length on top of me. I wrapped both my arms and legs around her. She ran the short wave of hair at my temple gently through her fingers.

"Wow," she whispered.

In reply I kissed her lips.

"Here, let me get in next to you," she said after a moment. She shimmied her hips to the side and I shifted to let her lie against me, her back pressed hard against the cushioned backrest. She held me tight with one leg, an arm thrown across my chest.

I turned my head to press my nose to hers, running my thumbprint down her cheek.

Then I leaned back and scrabbled on the floor, dragging up our jackets and using them to cover us. I snuggled happily back down and wrapped her in my arms again.

"Well," she said, smiling.

"Well, well, well," I said, grinning back.

"You comfy enough?"

"I'm sweet. But I'm half off this seat, so if you let me go I'll tumble to the floor."

She laughed and squeezed my shoulder. "I'll never let go, Jack. Hey, speaking of that movie" she reached up and dragged her hand down the window.

I craned my neck to see the handprint and chuckled. "Oh geez, we steamed your bus up pretty good. We'll have to give it a wipe."

"No way! I can play dumb—'Oh *my*, how *did* that Kate Winslet-looking handprint get there?'—See?"

"Wowee! Call up the Golden Globes we've got a new nominee." I chuckled, but as I ran my hand down her hip and brought it to rest on her firm backside, my stomach clenched and I sensed a cold feeling at the top of my spine.

Lying here, holding her close, and feeling her warm breath against my cheek, was *too* good almost. Hell, even the smell of her sweat was sweetly familiar and made my throat tighten.

"Christine, I…" I fell silent. Yet again I had started talking without thinking about what I was going to say.

She lifted my mouth to hers with a gentle touch of her fingertips on my cheek and kissed me. It turned me on all over again.

"Hey," she still held my face close to hers and spoke softly. "You're right that this could cause problems for the both of us. You know I never make rash decisions but, I guess, this didn't even feel like a decision. It's like you came back into my life and a big tornado's come and whisked me up. Right up into the sky."

"So what happens next?" I tried to keep my voice low and steady, but there was a tell-tale waver.

She exhaled slowly and her eyebrows knitted together. "I have no idea. Do you know?"

I flicked through scenarios in my mind. Meeting up for a date in Auckland if we were both there at the same time? Impossible. The World Cup training and playing schedule was already gruelling enough. And I couldn't imagine telling my teammates. Coach had sat us down at the last training camp and talked to us about the mindset we'd need for the tournament. How, for the few weeks of the World Cup, we would have to be the most mentally disciplined we had ever been. Her words echoed in my head now—"No distractions."

Christine raised her eyebrows as she waited for me to respond. My chest swelled as I looked at her, my head rested on her shoulder and her face inches from mine.

I covered her breast with my hand, stroking the nipple slowly with my thumb. "I don't know either."

"Hey, now," she said, putting her hand on mine to give me a firmer press on her boob, "don't give me those sad puppy-dog eyes. I've got your number. I'll check our schedules. Maybe we can get a seedy hotel room sometime before this is all over."

I smiled as the damp weight in my belly dispersed. "Okay. But does it have to be seedy? Aren't you making that Reebok money?"

She rolled me onto my back and sat back up on my stomach, pinning my hands above my head. "Oh, I see! I see. You'll fuck me on a manky-ass backseat of a hired bus, covered in spilt Gatorade and the crumbs of protein bars, but you're too good for an economically priced hotel that you for some reason assume I'm paying for?"

My eyebrows shot up. "Of course you're paying. And you said this was a very clean bus!"

"It is, it is. I'm kidding. You're lucky you're cute, McGee." She kissed me, slowly but deeply. Her pussy started to rub back and forth just below my navel.

She sat up. "Damn. You're going to get me going again." She traced a slow line down my collarbone and between my breasts, following its progress with her eyes. Then her gaze met mine and she pressed her lips together. "But I've got to get back. My roomie's going to think I've been kidnapped by the Canadians." She kissed me on the cheek, the corner of her mouth lingering on mine for a second. She started to climb off me, and every inch of my skin cried out from the loss of her.

I clutched her thighs to stop her moving. She looked at me quickly, then I relented and raised my hands like a criminal surrendering.

I stood up too. "You're right. Fletch has probably already sent out a search party."

I picked up an article of clothing. I held it up to my face and ascertained it was Christine's shirt. With a grin I swapped it for the bra she had in her hand.

"You're rooming with them? Have they fully recovered from that shoulder injury?"

"That's enough spy games from you, James Bond," I said, chucking her bra at her so it landed on her head. "They're fit and firing, thank you very much. How about Greta Finlay's knee? Is she back to a full training load yet?"

"All right, all right. You keep your secrets and I'll keep mine. You played really well yesterday, by the way."

I grinned and sat down next to her to put my socks back on. "Hey, thanks. You had a great game too."

"Well, aren't we just a picture of sportsmanship?"

Both fully dressed we pressed up next to each other way closer than the empty bus warranted.

Christine grabbed her phone from her pocket and unlocked it. "Yikes, eleven messages. I'll have to run."

"Can I have your phone for a sec," I asked.

She handed it to me. "Is this some kind of trust exercise? I don't hand my unlocked phone over to anyone. Not even Lori."

I scoffed. "Here," I held her phone up next to mine. "I've given us code names. I can't have my phone flashing up with a call from Christine Delacourt while I'm out with the team."

I'd put myself in as "Jack", and she was in my contacts under "Rose".

She smiled in the blue light from the screens, put her hand to my cheek and kissed my mouth. "I'm king of the world," she said. We both sighed as we stood up, and she led me by the hand back down toward the door.

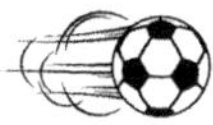

I arrived back at my hotel to a very worried Fletch, who thought I'd been attacked by feral quokkas while walking up Hay Street. I apologised profusely for being incommunicado for so long and explained there were no quokkas on the mainland. I told them my phone had died, but was betrayed when it very ostentatiously lit up in my hand at that very moment.

"Er, ah, looks like I just had it accidentally switched off." I slapped my forehead with my palm. "Silly old me. Sorry again, Fletch. But, as you can see, I'm safe and sound and free from quokka-rabies."

They scowled, punched their pillow a couple of times, then turned the bedside light off so I was left in darkness.

I closed the bathroom door behind me and fumbled to unlock my phone. The text was from 'Rose'. My chest fluttered.

I wish I'd drawn you like one of my French girls so I could see your body right now. I'm going to go to sleep now so I can dream about you.

I closed my eyes and leaned back against the door. I was turned on all over again.

I lifted my phone and my thumbs danced across my screen.

I just flooded my hull. Good night! I'll be dreaming about you too.

I stripped off and turned on the shower, twisting the taps so the water was a fair bit colder than I would usually have it.

It didn't help. I lay in bed later, curled up into a big ball of horniness. It took me a long time to fall asleep.

Chapter 14

My phone rang and started vibrating like a mini-jackhammer on the bedside table. I grabbed it then almost threw it across the room as my adrenaline spiked when I saw the name on the screen. Rose. I fumbled in my sheets trying to retrieve it.

"Shit, shit, shit, shit." I hit the green button to answer. "Hello? Hello! Yes!"

Christine laughed quietly and low. God, it was sexy. "Hey there. Did I wake you?"

"No! Well, yes. You did. Sorry, I don't know why I just lied then. I don't make a habit of it."

"Glad to hear it."

I looked around. My room, back in Melbourne. When I was travelling a lot it sometimes took me a bit to figure out where I was when I woke up in the morning. It was two days since the bus. I grinned as the memory of that night flooded back.

"Sorry I didn't get a chance to phone you yesterday," Christine said. "I would have if there was any way. But you know what recovery days are like."

"No worries," I said, trying to sound as chill as possible—like I hadn't been waiting, my thumb hovering over my phone screen, until the cabin crew on our Perth to Melbourne flight had said we could switch our devices off airplane mode. My stomach had sunk when no missed calls or texts had come through.

I opened my mouth to speak but snapped it shut again. What should I say? I was full to the brim with feelings. Happiness and still a little bit of shock at having hooked up with Christine again out of the blue; low-key horniness at the sounds of her voice coming down the phone; and a longing to see her face and her smile again.

Also, when she wasn't right in front of me, it was easier to give in to the flashes of doubt about whether I was ready to trust her again. The sound of her voice was keeping them at bay right now, though. I cleared my throat. "So, uh, how are you?" I winced. *The opposite of smooth!*

"Oh! Yeah. Good." It was her turn to clear her throat. "I feel really, um, glad. You know, glad about the other night. With you."

I let out a laugh.

"Sorry, was that a weird thing to say?" she asked.

"No! Not at all. I'm just so…glad too. I was glad that you're glad. And I never realised what a crazy word 'glad' is, now that I'm saying it so much."

She laughed too.

I breathed out and relaxed, relieved that Christine seemed to feel at least a little bit of what I'd been feeling for the last day and a bit.

"How's Perth?" I asked.

"Wouldn't know. We took the red-eye. I'm in Melbourne right now."

My body thrilled. She was so much closer than I thought! "Wow! Really?"

"Yeah, the team managers think putting us on a plane soon after the match will give us more time to prepare for the next match, compared to travelling later. Which might give us an advantage? I dunno. I feel wrecked right now, but I guess the experts know what they're doing."

"Totally. Hey, I wish I could see you." My mind whizzed around with possibilities. A short Uber ride and Christine could be here, with me, in my bed. I was shot through with a jolt of electricity just thinking about it. But there wasn't any feasible way I could sneak her in without Fletch and Viv knowing. It was too big a risk.

"I want to see you too, Keeley. I was actually thinking, and this is crazy—did you want to meet me out somewhere?"

"But what about top secrecy? Melbourne is a sports-mad town. People will recognise you, and as far as anyone knows you're still with Cora." Plus I was still on thin ice with my team following Dumpstergate. Coach had told me to pull my head in, and being seen out canoodling with a star opponent would definitely be viewed as the type of distraction I was meant to be avoiding.

"I hear you. But what if there were no people?"

I scrunched up my face. "Nope, you've lost me. I have no idea what you're on about."

She chuckled. "You really were fast asleep when I phoned you, hey? Look outside."

I swung my bare legs out of the covers and gasped as my skin turned to instant gooseflesh. I grabbed my quilt and swathed it over my head like a wizard's cloak as I padded the couple of steps across the carpet and drew the heavy curtain aside.

"Holy shit," I said. A neatly trimmed pin oak on the other side of the street was bent at a crazy diagonal by a strong wind. The sky was heavy and grey, and sleet flew through the air in freezing gusts.

"I know, right? I thought Seattle had shit weather, but it looks like Melbourne's is worse."

"I thought the swirling, whooshing noise was Fletch vacuuming. They get into cleaning mode in the lead-up to big games."

"Look, I know this is asking a lot. Too much. I don't want to jeopardise your match prep or your health. But I'm up here in my hotel looking at the deserted waterfront below me, and I can't help thinking we have the chance to be alone. In plain sight, you know? Even just for a few minutes. Actually, it sounds nuts now I'm saying it. It's totally fine if you want to say no."

I put the phone on speaker and chucked it down on the bed, pulling on the first shirt I grabbed from my chest of drawers. "I'm on my way. Find us a spot and drop me a pin in Maps."

"Yes, awesome," she said. The warmth and happiness in her voice made me even more certain I was making the right choice.

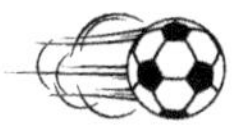

"Just here is fine," I said to my Uber driver.

"Are you sure?" he replied as another gust of sleet whoomped against the car. He squinted up at the dark grey sky through the windscreen, maybe wondering if he would be liable if I got out of his car and was immediately whisked skywards like Dorothy and Toto.

I tapped to give him the maximum tip (danger money for the abysmal conditions), crammed my phone deep into a pocket of my waterproof jacket and got out of the warmth and safety of the car, quickly closing the door behind me.

I leaned into the wind as I crossed the grassy open space between the road and the St Kilda beachfront. I was lucky I had some serious cold-weather gear from my time playing in Sweden. I was done up as if I was going skiing, with a puffy hooded jacket and matching pants.

A lone figure was sitting inside a big wooden rotunda ahead of me. I scanned St Kilda Esplanade in either direction. The usually calm ocean was roiled up and crashing against the stone wall that separated the narrow beach from the walkway lined with giant palm trees. Not another soul in sight.

I reached the rotunda and climbed the couple of steps. The person at the far end stood and raised their hand in greeting. I walked so quickly forward that it was almost a skip.

"It *is* you, thank goodness," I said.

She grinned and wrapped her arms around me. "No one else would be dumb enough to be outdoors on a day like this."

I squeezed her and pressed my lips to hers. "I don't feel dumb. I actually feel very clever."

She kissed me and despite the weather I felt a warm glow, like everything was right with the world.

She pressed her hand to the side of my face. "You're so puffy, I can hardly get my arms around you," she said.

I grinned. "Yeah, I've dressed for an Everest hike." I looked down. "Cripes! You're pretty much just in sweats! Aren't you cold?"

"A little. I told my roommate Mikayla I was just going down to the lobby to read. It would have looked a little strange if I had then proceeded to put a snowsuit on."

"Holy Moses, Chrissie! You've got to get better at lying. Your teeth are chattering. Here." I unzipped my big jacket and wrapped her up in it, pulling her against me. "Legs too." I plonked down on the wooden floor, steering Christine so she was sitting with her back against my chest. She drew her knees up and I wrapped my legs around her as best I could. I pulled my jacket tighter around her so we were both inside it, and rested my chin on her shoulder.

"Better?" I asked.

She sighed and leaned back against me. The muscles in her shoulders relaxed and she stopped shivering. I squeezed my eyes shut and pressed my lips against her jawline at the edge of her hoodie.

She exhaled shakily. "I wanted this," she said. "I wanted you. Even though it's completely crazy to be out here in this stupid, freezing-ass, Melbourne-freaking-weather." She took hold of my wrists where they crossed in front of her and pressed my arms more firmly around her. Her cheek scrunched where mine rested against it as she smiled. "It's not a smart decision to be out here with you. Not smart but, you know, good. Perfect."

I got such a rush of tenderness for her I felt like I might start crying. I took a deep breath and held it together. "I guess there are more important things than smart decisions."

"You're the only person, in my whole entire life, that has made me feel that. Everyone's always like, 'Work hard, no mistakes, don't miss your shot.' Well, Lori doesn't either. She's always telling me to chill the fuck out."

I chuckled. "That sounds like Lori."

We sat in silence for a little while, watching the grey sea roiling all the way to the dark horizon.

"That's what drew me to you way back at the start," she said quietly. "You *enjoyed* everything—soccer, eating pizza with Naomi and those girls, long bus rides to play in Atlanta blasting Taylor Swift on repeat the whole way. There was nothing behind it. I remember wanting to ask if I could borrow some of that from you, like a cup of sugar. Or wrap myself up in you."

I smiled. "Kind of like now?"

"Exactly like now."

I closed my eyes and cast my mind back. "I remember thinking how your drive and intensity kind of radiated off you. I couldn't ignore it when I was around you. At first it threw me. But then..."

"I whomped you enough with it that you gave in?"

"No, not that. I realised I wanted you to turn that intensity toward me."

"And I did."

"And it was awesome."

"Until it wasn't." She turned her face away from mine just a little. "I'm sorry. I know I'm tough to be with."

Sorry. I turned the word over in my mind. In the couple of years after she left I had wanted an apology—had felt the lack of one. And this wasn't really it. I couldn't take this throw-away line and run with it like she was making amends for how unfeeling and deceptive she had been all those years ago. Did I need that? Should I demand it?

I cleared my throat. "About that..." My skin burned, and I wanted to jump out of it. I hated uncomfortable conversations. "When we got un-awesome. It's just, um, I never understood. I still don't."

She didn't reply right away and looked out to sea. "When I look back, I can't believe how wrong I got it. I really, really messed it up. I convinced myself I was protecting you by not telling you about Seattle, that I was putting you first. I've realised how insane that is. Patronising, even. Like I'm the expert in interpersonal relationships." She scoffed, then craned her neck back to look at me. "But I was being selfish and chicken shit. I'm truly sorry."

I ran my thumb gently down her lips. "It's okay." Her apology didn't completely erase the memory of the hurt she'd caused me, but the doubts swirling around in the back of my head eased.

I breathed in the scent of her skin. The wind the rain and the sea stormed and raged together like they would never stop.

We sat for a while longer, her bundled up in my jacket, chatting about nothing in particular—books we'd read, movies we wanted to see.

My legs started to get pins and needles from sitting on the hard floor, but I held onto her as long as she would let me.

Chapter 15

We won our next match against South Korea. Half the teams in the tournament had to pack their bags and go home, but those lucky enough to remain were getting ready to play off in the Round of Sixteen.

We were in Adelaide, a smaller city I liked a lot. There were good cafes and you could see the sometimes stark but always picturesque Adelaide Hills from the very centre of the city because they'd designed it as a grid of wide boulevards. Plus, practically all Adelaideans were sports mad, so I could chat with anyone.

Christine and I had been texting a lot, and had managed to talk on the phone every evening. I thanked heavens my teammates knew I took a little solo walk most nights, so nobody was suspicious when I took off for some alone time.

Tonight Coach had said that, instead of team dinner at the hotel, we could have a free evening to do whatever we wanted. Fletch knew the city better than I did, so I had them take me to their favourite place—an Ethiopian restaurant in West Hindmarsh. The red lentil curry eaten with a big shared sour flatbread called injera had been amazing, and we had the Uber drop us a short distance from our hotel so we could walk in the fresh air, full and happy.

My phone rang. 'Rose'. I hit the green button to answer.

"Hi!" I said brightly. "Would you mind if I called you back in ten minutes?"

Christine chuckled. "You sound like you're not quite at liberty to talk privately?"

"Yes, Adelaide. It's been good so far."

She dropped her voice to a whisper. "I want to push you up against the nearest wall and stick my head under your T-shirt."

"Sounds good. Uh-huh, talk to you then. Take care. Bye!" I hung up.

Fletch looked at me sideways. "Who was that?"

"Uhhhhhh...Viv! Vivienne. She said I got a letter from the Footscray Library and she was wondering if I needed any overdue books returned."

"Oh, why didn't you just talk to her now? I wouldn't have minded speaking to her for a bit too."

"Ohhhhhh, yeah? Yes! I should have. I'm trying to live a bit more... 'in the moment' you know. If I'm spending time with you, I'm spending time with *you*. Mindfulness."

They shoved their hands in their pockets against the dry cold wind and walked a little faster. "Yeah, I get it."

I trotted a few steps to catch up. I pressed my phone to my chest and smiled. No wind off the Nullarbor Plain was going to stop me from finding a secluded corner outside the hotel. I would have Christine's sweet voice in my ear in a couple of minutes.

I said good-bye to Fletch at the door and walked around the side of the building to a bench under a low awning. The ground was scattered with cigarette butts and I figured this spot was frequented by hotel staff. I phoned Christine.

"Hi there." Her voice had a smile in it.

"Hi yourself. Sorry about before."

"No, I'm sorry. I thought your team time would be well and truly over by now."

"You forget Adelaide's behind Melbourne. It's earlier here. You weren't far off though. I was just walking back to the hotel with Fletch."

"And were they fooled by your quick-thinking improvisation?"

"Oh yeah, I just said you were Viv."

"Viv! What a sweetie."

"She really is. Hey, she's not far from you, you know. Our house is just a couple of suburbs away from the city."

"Look, she's the greatest. But it's not her I want to see."

I hugged my middle. My chest and arms tingled with how much I wanted to hold Christine. "I would love to take you to my house. We could order food and not come out of the bedroom for days."

She breathed into the phone. "That would be amazing. I wish you were here with me now."

"Me too."

She was silent for a beat. "Keeley, I was thinking today that I felt different. I meditated on it and realised, well, I've been lonely for a long time. Even with Cora, I felt lonely. But now, since Perth, I don't. I miss you, but I'm not lonely."

I closed my eyes as a warm golden glow ran down from the top of my head. "I'm not as good at meditation as you, but I do have Viv. She's been telling me there's been something missing. I thought she was wrong, but now I realise she was right. Only there's not anything missing now."

"I wish I could kiss you." Her voice was thick.

"I want you too. Are we going to be in the same city again soon?"

"I've been looking at the draw. It depends." There was a rustle of paper. "If you beat Italy then win your next match, probably against China, you might be in Sydney for the semis. We might cross over before we leave for our semi in Auckland."

"I love how it's *if* Australia makes the semis, and *when* the US makes the semis."

She laughed. "If you want to run with the best in the world, you gotta keep up."

I scoffed. "Yeah, yeah, yeah. Keep a lid on it, Delacourt."

She did not seem to accept the possibility of losing when it came to herself but was comfortable enough with the idea of me losing. I wondered how badly it would shake her up if I were to win and she were to lose. Her most recent relationship had been with a very successful athlete, and it had fallen apart.

"Hey," she said, the smile dropping out of her voice. "You know I'm all in for this Cup. You get it, it's been my dream and it's crazy that it's coming true day by day."

I sat up straighter. "I get it. There's not that many people in the world who get it as much as I do."

"Well… damn, what am I trying to say? I can't look past these next few weeks. All the sports psychs working with us say we've got to stay present and mindful. If I think about life after the final match, my focus starts to skitter away and I lose my centre."

My insides lilted sideways. She was managing my expectations of her. Already—six days in. I clamped down on the feeling. "Wow. 'Psychs' plural. The Australian Institute of Sport only sent my team one."

"Keeley."

I unclenched the fist I hadn't realised I'd made and flexed my fingers a few times. If Viv were here she'd accuse me of 'deflecting with humour' and I would be guilty as charged.

And I'd been doing the exact same as Christine in my head. If my thoughts skipped ahead like a smooth rock in a creek, I'd let it sink and think instead about that night on the bus, or something sweet to text her as soon as I could. The future was too many questions that would take a whole heap of work to answer. And soccer was the central focus at the moment. The tournament was more than half over. What was another handful of days?

I bit my bottom lip. "I understand. I feel good, talking to you right this minute. That's all that matters."

"You're amazing, you know that? You remember that first night we were together, after the NCAA final? We slept all cuddled up in that little bed."

"I remember. Of course!"

"I didn't tell you this at the time, but I hadn't slept for more than two hours at a stretch since I'd left home for college. That was the best night's sleep I'd had in a very long while."

"Whoa. I remember you were usually strung tighter than a high-toned cello, but I didn't know you were that bad."

"I was bad. Anxious, homesick—probably a nightmare to be around. But falling asleep with you wrapped around me that night, I actually let go and let the peace in. I felt safe with you."

"I remember I tried to stay awake because I didn't want to miss a moment. Like that old Aerosmith song from that space movie. I didn't know how long it would last or when it would happen again." *Kind of like now.*

"I think I've heard that song, but I never knew who sings it. All old white rock-guys look the same to me."

I laughed.

We stayed talking until my bum went numb against the hard seat. The skin around my fingernails looked a little blue and I had to fight to stop my teeth from chattering.

I ran into the hotel foyer to escape the wind, calculating that it was about twenty-two hours until I could hear her voice again. I was probably the only person on my team who wasn't thinking about our next game.

Our (only) sports psych Harriet always told us not to play the game in our heads in the lead-up to a big match. It didn't help and could burn you out mentally before you even took to the pitch. But was my focus too far away from winning games with my team? Christine had told me in no uncertain terms that she wasn't going to let this thing we were doing throw her off *her* game.

Soccer was number one in her life, until someone lifted that World Cup trophy above their heads and the fireworks went off.

And after that? I pictured myself at the edge of a creek, running my thumb over a perfectly smooth stone. I didn't toss it though. I bounced on the balls of my feet as I waited for the lift to arrive.

I had to think of some story to give Fletch about what Viv and I could have possibly been talking about for eighty-six minutes.

Chapter 16

"I HAVE STRICT INSTRUCTIONS TO bring you back to the hotel straight after the event ends," said our team publicist, Brianna.

"What! Why?" asked Allie.

"Coach's orders."

Brianna was driving me, Allie and Ava to a media event to mark the halfway point of the World Cup. A few players from each of the remaining teams had been invited to a fancy party at the Sydney Opera House. We were stuck in evening traffic, moving at a crawl down Pitt Street toward the harbour.

Allie swung around to look at me in the back seat and narrowed her eyes. "Could it have something to do with Coach wanting to avoid more drama with someone and their ex?"

I tensed up so hard my head whacked against the seat back. Christine was going to be there tonight. "Who, uhhhh, what…?"

"Amber Hatfield is going to be there to sing that tournament anthem song. Don't tell me you didn't know. I clocked you texting all day with a dumb grin on your face."

"Oh, her." I exhaled and felt for my phone in my pocket. I fought the urge to pull it out to check if I had any more messages from Christine.

"Yeah, Keels. Try not to jump into any bins tonight," Ava said, laughing.

Brianna's intense focus on the road ahead made me suspect Allie had been right about the motivation behind the new rule.

I stuck my bottom lip out and watched pedestrians move down the block way faster than us in our brand new, powerful electric car on loan from a tournament sponsor. "I didn't jump *in* the bin—I jumped *on* the bin," I muttered.

When we finally arrived a valet took our car and Brianna ushered us up the Opera House steps. The big white sails of the building had a massive soccer ball and the tournament logo projected onto them.

A bank of photographers asked us to stop and smile for them at the entrance. The three of us stood grinning in our matching team polos and nice slacks.

Then Brianna stepped in and herded us inside. "We've got canapes and drinks here in the foyer for the next thirty minutes. No alcohol. Be nice to everyone who talks to you—the main point of tonight is to give the sponsors a chance to feel a part of it all. Anyone you talk to might be the CEO of a major multi-national corporation."

"Oh good. Is the head of Samsung here? My TV's on the blink and I don't know how to fix it," I said.

Brianna didn't dignify me with a response. "Then I'll come and fetch you and we'll go backstage. There'll be a speech and then Amber Hatfield will sing the tournament song and after that you'll all come out on stage for photos. They'll want plenty of footage for social media promos, so you might be there a few minutes. I'll check with the organisers if they want more video content, but if not we're straight back to the hotel."

I spotted my friend Lotta who played for Sweden and waved. "Drink lots of alcohol, scowl in photos, get home late. Got it. Bye," I said, then headed off toward a trio of Swedes in their bright blue and yellow polos.

We chatted for a bit and I scanned the room in search of Christine. I had a good excuse to look around—the foyer had towering walls of glass revealing views of the Harbour Bridge lit up in all its glory. The city looked spectacular with countless lights shimmering off the water.

The Swedish version of Brianna came and told my companions that they needed to come and chat with some ambassador.

"Been a while since you took me to a party," said a voice at my shoulder. My body thrilled and I swung around. Christine stood at a respectable distance, holding a drink in front of her with both hands.

"Hey," I said.

"Hey yourself."

We both stood with half-smiles on our faces. Underneath I was struggling though. We'd talked about seeing each other, and how we'd have to keep it cool. Brianna or my teammates could be watching me right now, and I'd have a lot of explaining to do if I gave in to the urge to dash Christine's soda water to the floor and make out with her then and there.

"It's good to see you," I said. I wanted to look at every inch of her at once. She was dressed the same as me, but the polo was navy and white instead of forest-green and gold. And nobody in the history of the world has ever looked sexier in a polyester shirt with a logo on it.

Someone tapped me on the shoulder and said my name loudly. Christine raised an eyebrow at me and walked off with a half-smile. I swung around to see a woman and man who looked as if they were in their sixties.

"Hello?" I said. I tried to keep the question mark and also the irritation out of my voice, but failed at both. The pair didn't seem to mind though. They launched smilingly into a spiel about how they'd love my autograph for their daughter Shiloh at home, who had posters of me plastered all over her wall.

I smiled and nodded, wondering how quickly I could get out of this interaction. Brianna's instructions were out the window—the couple could be number one on Forbes' rich list and be about to offer me unlimited use of their private island, but I only wanted to find Christine again. Looking at her face from a socially acceptable distance was torture, but not looking at her was worse.

The woman pulled a pen and a rolled-up A3 poster of me out of her handbag and watched as I signed it.

"Oh, she'll be thrilled, really thrilled," she said.

It struck me they looked a little old to have a kid at home, but you can never rule out a last-minute miracle.

"Does she play?" I asked. If I knew a kid played, I would usually write something like 'keep kicking goals.'

The woman tittered. "Oh, no. Shiloh hasn't played for twenty years!"

"Twenty—? Wait on, how old is she?"

"Twenty-nine and three quarters," said Shiloh's dad. He pulled out a notepad from his top jacket pocket, flipped a couple of pages and read. "She said to tell you could you please follow her back on Insta so she can slide into your DMs. Oh, and that she's single." He put the notepad back in his pocket and looked at me expectantly.

I opened and shut my mouth a couple of times but nothing came out. This conversation had slid sideways into a very weird place and I'd been left behind. "Uhh…"

Brianna appeared at Shiloh's mum's shoulder. "So sorry to interrupt. Keeley, it's time for you to head backstage."

"Oh, shoot!" I said. "Well, wouldn't you know it. And we were having such a nice chat. So lovely to meet you both. Bye now."

"But! We didn't tell you Shiloh's Instagram profile handle," said her mum.

"Don't you worry," I said over my shoulder as we moved away. "I'll do an algorithm search for her on the engine."

"What was that all about?" asked Brianna.

"Nothing. They were just warning me about someone I should definitely block on all my socials."

Backstage, a woman dressed in black and wearing a chunky headset talked to us in a loud whisper. There were about fifty players assembled around her, straining to hear.

"The lights are about to go down," she hissed. "Wait here in silence during the speeches and musical performance, then file out onto the stage at *my signal.*" She lifted her arm straight up into the air and waved a few times in a sweeping motion as if directing a plane taxiing down the runway.

I turned a full circle looking for Christine in the press of people. No luck. I craned my neck and stood up on tiptoes but just then the lights went out. Our backstage airport conductor stood closest to the curtains at the side of the stage and was faintly illuminated but everyone else was in darkness. Someone launched into a speech out on the stage.

I clenched my fists at my sides. It was so frustrating to know Christine was so close but not be able to get to her.

There was movement beside me and an arm brushed against mine.

I whipped my head around and strained to make out who it was. I felt her there before my eyes adjusted. *Christine.* The anxiety and helplessness I had felt melted away and were replaced with a warm solidity. This feeling—as much as her shape and her smell—was how I knew she was there with me.

She leaned toward me and whispered so quietly the people around us wouldn't have been able to hear it over their own breathing. "Come with me."

She started to walk backwards, smoothly moving around the other women in our big group. I took a step backwards right onto someone's foot and earned a hissed "Watch it!" in an English accent.

I kept moving until I felt a brick wall at my back. Christine gently entwined her fingers in mine. I fought not to gasp as heat lashed through me from the points where her skin touched mine.

She led me by the hand a few steps, and we brushed past a heavy black curtain. It was even darker on the other side.

Christine put her fingers to my chin and guided my face toward hers. When her lips met mine I got so turned on I felt like I couldn't breathe. I kissed her slowly so no movement would alert the other players standing on the other side of the curtain. I pressed my body against her, overcome by the feel and smell and taste of her that I had been craving.

There was a muted rustle and scrape of feet against the floor. We let go of each other and went back through the curtain. My breath and body had a second ago been connected with her, and now I was cold and alone. And turned on. *Oh shit.*

I hurried to catch up with the group. I squinted as I emerged last from the curtains and the auditorium's lights hit me. *Am I walking funny?* I was intensely aware of the pressure between my legs.

The audience was clapping. I couldn't remember Brianna's instructions. Smile? Wave? Start a conga line and take it all the way to Kings Cross?

A woman in a shiny dress walked past me then paused. "Hi Keeley," she whispered.

"Huh? Uh, hi…Amber?" What was she doing there? Then it clicked. She must have just sung her song. I'd been too busy to hear a single note of it.

She turned and walked backwards a couple of steps and she reached the curtains. "You're meant to be one step back and two to your right."

"Shit! Ta." People with massive cameras rigged up on elaborate contraptions connected to their bodies performed all kinds of manoeuvres around us. We were spread out in two lines across the stage. It must have been very boring for the audience.

I leaned forward to try to spot Christine in one of the lines. Headset woman groaned from backstage, pointed toward the camera in front of me, then gestured at a manically overdone smile on her own face.

I looked down the barrel and tried to smile. It was no good. Every single person of the hundreds in this room was standing in the way of me continuing to make out with Christine. Well at least I wouldn't be invited to the next stupid social media event because my scowl kept shitting on all the organisers' content.

Finally there was another round of applause and Headset Woman motioned for us to leave the stage. We followed her through a corridor then back out into the foyer. I couldn't kiss Christine again, but maybe we could stand in loaded awkward silence for a couple of minutes before Brianna bundled me into the car. I stood on my tiptoes and spotted her making her way toward me. I glowed inwardly. Her eyes met mine and she smiled. She was almost close enough to touch when a purple shape blocked her from my view.

"What the…?" I said.

"Hello, stranger."

"Amber."

She narrowed her eyes for a second but her arch smile didn't falter. "You don't sound happy to see me."

"No! I mean, sorry. You just kind of came out of nowhere. Are you wearing a different dress from three minutes ago?" I leaned very slightly to my right to look over her shoulder.

Christine was standing there with her back to us. By the set of her shoulders and the turn of her head I could tell she was listening in to this exchange.

My glow was replaced with a sick feeling. Precious seconds were ticking past!

"But of course. Any ole person can sing, but super-quick costume changes are what makes a true popstar. Do you like it? I think I look like Ronald McDonald's friend Grimace. But high fashion of course."

I looked straight at her. I was going to have to get rid of her. "It's something all right. Hey, would it be okay—"

"I know you've been busy playing, but I was kind of hoping I'd hear from you since you've been in Sydney so much."

"Oh, er, they keep us on a pretty tight leash."

"Totally. I get it." She rested her hand on my forearm. "Maybe we could have lunch next time you're in town?"

My mind raced. It would be quickest to throw out a 'yeah, sure' and move on from the question. But I couldn't. I couldn't stand there with Christine within earshot and make a date with another woman—no matter how much of a lie my promise was, and how loose the commitment. A pressure built in my chest.

"I'm sorry but I'm not going to be able to agree to that at this point in time." The words tumbled out sounding thin and strangled.

Amber took her hand off my arm and laced her fingers together against her belly. "Is there someone else?" She didn't sound cold, or pissed. Just neutral. The absence of her usual playful archness was notable. She just wanted to know the answer.

The pressure in my chest rose to my throat. "Yes."

She nodded and all at once the smile was back. "Story of my life. Good for you. They must be quite something to be able to reel you in, Keeley."

I nodded. She pulled me into a big hug and pressed her lips to my cheek before walking off.

Christine turned.

Brianna stepped in front of me. “Keeley! You were meant to come find me. The others are already in the car.” She marched a couple of steps then turned to make sure I was following.

I threw my head back then headed off after her. Even though walking away from Christine felt awful and I knew this would make it even harder, I looked over my shoulder.

As she stood watching me go, she mouthed two words. *Thank you.*

Chapter 17

I HAD A TOURNAMENT REST day in Brisbane before our quarter-final match. My hometown Logan was only a half-hour drive from the middle of Brisbane city, so I was excited that about a dozen of my friends and family were able to come to the next day's game.

Viv was flying up from Melbourne for the match too. She was staying with my parents overnight. Over the years since I was a college freshman they had come to regard Viv as a second daughter, and always said they could never repay how well she'd looked after me. One Christmas my mum had told us it was her dearest wish that the two of us would end up together. I'd nearly choked on my slice of baked ham and shouted, "Ew!"

Viv had calmly explained that, after so many years, we loved each other like sisters.

I'd asked for a leave pass to stay in Logan too, but Coach said I had to stay with the team in the hotel. I reminded myself the World Cup was only for another two weeks. I could take a decent break and visit home afterwards.

I was spending the morning of my precious rest day at a media event in front of Brisbane's City Hall, along with teammates who happened to be from anywhere in the state of Queensland. The five of us were lined up in our team polos and slacks, and in front of each of us was a member of the Daisy Hill United Under-7s girls soccer team, in full kit and cleats, hair ribbons resplendent in team colours. The organisers had got it right—the photos and footage were going to be adorable.

I'd have to send some photos to Christine. She might not get this news story where she was, in Auckland, today. I grinned thinking about her. Luckily, we were all meant to be smiling for the cameras, so I didn't look too bizarre.

I clenched my hand a couple of times and tried to focus in on the here and now. It was something Coach tried to drum into us, to stop us getting caught up in the whirlwind of the tournament and burning out.

Some politician lady was at a lectern in front of us giving a speech about blazing pathways for the superstars of tomorrow. I looked past her and caught sight of Viv in the throng of people gathered in King George Square. Even in the very middle of winter the square was glary and hot. Some genius had decided to pave the whole thing in very light grey slate. I knew for a fact it was instant sunburn to spend a minute there in high summer.

I waved to Viv with both hands.

She frowned and shook her head.

I rolled my eyes. *Fine.* The stage was a sacred arena and I needed to nail my performance as a proud Aussie salt-of-the-earth sportswoman. I stretched a grin across my face and turned ever so slightly to show the crowd my right-hand profile, then my left, then back to my right, giving my best impression of a Miss Universe contestant being introduced, not by name but by geographical origin.

Viv scowled at me with such venom that I stopped, which was probably for the best.

Once the formalities were done I hung around to sign some posters and take selfies with the Daisy Hill United Under-7s and anyone else who was interested.

Viv sidled up beside me.

"Hey," I said, pulling her into a one-armed hug. "The organisers told us five more minutes. They don't want to pay these security guards for any longer than that."

"No sweat."

I posed for a selfie with each arm around a woman in a Melbourne Victory T-shirt. On the front they'd screen-printed the words "It's McGee for me!"

After a very brief chat with these mega-fans followed by a handful of other people, security started moving the crowd along. I headed off with Viv toward the big portico at the front of City Hall.

I caught sight of the politician who had given the speech walking toward Ann Street where a dark car waited for her, an old bloke in a suit standing ready to open the rear door. A short-haired woman in a dark-blue pants suit and rainbow lanyard approached her holding a sandwich wrapped in greaseproof paper.

The politician smiled as she approached, wrapped her arms around her shoulders, and kissed her on the mouth. Then she took the sandwich from her and kissed her again on the cheek as they walked toward the car together.

Unbidden a mini-daydream played in my head—Christine and me walking down the street hand-in-hand to our favourite brunch place (her usual order was an egg-white omelette and a double ristretto); me taking a time out from match preparation to drape the stars and stripes around my shoulders and cheer her on at the Olympics; at Logan Ikea checkouts, laughing together at all the other couples who didn't make it through the hell-maze without having a massive fight.

"Aw," I said.

"What?" Viv had walked past me into the marble-floored foyer and was moving in the direction of the entrance to the ballroom auditorium. She gravitated toward performance spaces anywhere she went.

I took her arm to arrest her natural momentum. "That politician who gave the speech just had her nice missus bring her a sandwich and gave her a big kiss."

"Aw. That's sweet. You never clock that stuff."

I shrugged. "I guess I'm going soft in my old age. Hey, it looks like the adoring fans have dispersed. Shall we luncheon?"

"Yes, let's," she replied in an excellent posh accent. She was in rehearsals to play Truly Scrumptious in *Chitty Chitty Bang Bang* at the Ballarat Regents Theatre.

I cleared my throat as we entered the mall on Adelaide Street. "Hey, um, if Fletch asks, can you say I've been talking to you on the phone for at least an hour every day?"

Viv stopped walking and hooked me by the elbow so I swung around to face her. "Oh, I can lie. If I can convince an audience of seven hundred people that I'm a doll on a music box, then I sure as hell can deceive Fletch—the sweetest, most trusting soul in the world, *Keeley.* You're going to have to tell me why."

I winced.

She eyeballed me, her mouth in a stern line.

I couldn't meet her gaze and my shoulders slumped. Who was I kidding? I didn't have the strategy and planning skills to pull off an illicit affair. I should have told Fletch I was on the phone with someone they would never be able to corroborate my story with. Any damn one of the dozens, maybe hundreds, of people that I knew, and they didn't. My Aunt Candice who was teaching English in Ho Chi Minh and hardly ever came home, for example?

There was nothing for it.

"Okay, okay. But you have to swear this stays in the vault. I'm serious."

She nodded.

"I've been talking on the phone with Christine Delacourt a lot. We hooked up in Perth a few weeks ago."

Viv stiffened and her eyes widened remarkably. "Eeeeeeeee..."

She sounded like a stove-top kettle. A group of tourists walking into the Ugg boot shop turned in alarm.

"Shit, hey, Viv. Quit it." I tapped her on both her shoulders at once. I went to put my hand over her mouth but stopped because that was a bit aggressive.

She kept emitting the high-pitched noise.

I put my hands on her cheeks. "Viv! Your vocal chords! You've gotta save them for *Lovely Lonely Man.*"

She went silent immediately, then said low and slowly. "Thanks. My understudy Peg would love it if I came down with nodes just before the premiere." She grabbed my arm with both of hers and took off walking again, her head leaned toward me so she could whisper conspiratorially. "This is *huge*. What the hell! How have you kept this from me for so long? How did it happen? Was it amazing? I knew you always held a flame for her. Didn't I tell you?"

I beamed. It was great to be able to tell someone about us. Some evenings, until my phone rang and it was Christine on the other end, I felt like the whole thing was a sweaty fantasy I'd dreamt up. But it wasn't—it was a sweaty fantastic reality. "Oh, you know, it was chill. We happened to meet by moonlight next to the river, then she asked for my number and told me she'd been thinking about me. Then she texted to say she's broken up with that snowboarder, then she asked me to come to her hotel—don't start that shrieking thing again."

She clamped her mouth closed, going a bit pink from the effort of staying silent. Her hands on my arm were trembling. "How did you sneak past her teammates?" she asked in a strangled whisper.

"Well.... Ow!"

She had squeezed my arm like a vice. She loosened the grip. "Sorry."

"We didn't quite make it *into* the hotel. She had the keys of the team bus."

She gave a long and noisy gasp. "You despoiled the US women's national team *bus*? That...is...awesome! But..." She narrowed her eyes. "Is she treating you well? I know she's capable of it. She was sweet as pie the last time, right up until, you know." She mimed a pie being dropped from high above her head then splattering on the ground.

"She's great," I said.

"Awwww." Viv ruffled my hair. "Look at that grin. I'm dying. You know I've never seen anyone else have this effect on you. Maybe there's something special about Villain Christine after all."

"There's one small issue though. If we win tomorrow and the US win their quarter, it will be us versus the US in the semi-final. Sudden death."

To my surprise she shrugged and kept walking.

I spluttered. "Don't you think this is high drama? Her dreams, my dreams, on a collision course? Blood on the tracks?"

She scoffed. “You athletes are so caught up in your own stories. Do you think there’s not a theatre scene in the world where there’s not a couple vying for every male lead role? Auditions, rejections, watching their glory from side-of-stage. At the end of the day, it’s just a job.”

“Wow, Viv. That is really sensible.”

She rolled her eyes. “I’m sensible. Have the two of you talked it through?”

“Not exactly. I think we both just agreed that we would cross the bridge when we came to it. Why add more complications, when it may never happen? Even now it feels a bit dumb talking about it. We still need to beat Brazil and Christine still needs to beat England. Neither of those things will be easy.”

We started to climb the Charlotte Street hill toward the little tandoori place where we’d decided to have lunch. “So, what now? What next? You fell like a UFO into the New Mexico desert for her last time. There’s a big chance she’ll hurt you again. What’s the plan?”

An icy whisper of worry touched my skin, making the hairs on the back of my neck stand up. “When have you ever known me to have a plan, Viv? I’m taking this one day at a time—shit, even one hour at a time. If she leaves again, you’ll be there to pick up the pieces, hey?”

She rested her head against my shoulder. “Always. With tea and sympathy. And I could serenade you with the saddest songs from *West Side Story* if you like?”

I patted her hand. “The tea sounds great, mate.”

Chapter 18

We beat Brazil in a penalty shoot-out to get into the semi-final. Even the next day I couldn't believe it. My cheeks hurt from grinning. I might have grinned all night in my sleep. And sleep-punched the air and sleep-hi-fived support staff and fans.

The final moments of the match seemed like a daydream—a fantasy every soccer-loving kid has, of being tapped on the shoulder to take the deciding kick. And nailing it.

But this was real. After all the forwards had taken their shots with varying degrees of success, I stepped up fifth to take mine. If I got it, we won. Even my maths-averse brain could grasp that equation.

I did my normal routine: placed the ball's FIFA symbol facing me in the dead centre; took four steps back while taking two deep breaths—didn't block out the crowd noise but let it wash over me with calm curiosity, and fired the kick along the ground a hair's breadth inside the left goalpost.

A photo of me sprinting toward the crowd, my arms out like an aeroplane, with my entire team running full pelt after me whooping and throwing their arms around, made the front page of the Brisbane newspaper the following day. Fletch bought a whole stack of them from the Edward Street 7-Eleven and insisted on keeping them on their lap the entire flight to Sydney. We had a couple of rest days before we played our semi at Stadium Australia.

We greeted a few hardy fans waiting for us at Arrivals. Our plane had been an hour delayed taking off, which wasn't too awful for us in the Qantas lounge at the Brisbane Airport. It had given me a chance to trade a few texts with Christine. The US was playing a quarter final in Auckland the following evening.

My phone started vibrating in my pocket. I finished autographing a young kid's bright gold scarf, took a step back and grabbed my phone.

Christine!

"Hi Rosie Rose," I said. I spoke quietly but started beaming at the same time. Security started ushering us toward the big doors. I fell into line with my team.

"Hey there, Mrs Front Page."

"That's *Ms* Front Page to you. I'm a feminist."

"Oh, my sincerest apologies. Where are you?"

We crossed the road, then headed along a narrow, covered walkway toward a row of coaches. "At Sydney Airport. You?"

"Get out! *I'm* at Sydney airport."

"Get *out!* We're heading to our bus."

"We just pulled up. Hold on, wait… I freaking *see you!*"

"What?" I turned a full three-sixty.

Our goalie Sarah, who was walking behind me, nearly barrelled into me.

"Sorry!" I dropped my voice to barely above a whisper. "Hey, you might walk right by us. I've dropped to the back of the line."

"Yeah, yeah! I'll get off the bus last." She paused. "Hey, can you, like, get away?"

I craned my neck to look ahead at my whole squad and support staff. Could I fake a brutal attack of diarrhoea and run back to the terminal? No, it would never work—one security guy and probably Debbie our team doctor would rush back with me. And then what? Have Christine evade her whole team and sneak into a smelly bathroom stall so I could shove my hand down her tracksuit? Maybe Debbie would mistake sex noises for diarrhoea noises…?

I whisper-groaned. "No! Debbie would never buy it."

"Huh?"

"I would love to, Chrissie. You gotta know that, but we would never get away with it."

She sighed. "I know, I know. It was a crazy idea. I just want you. You know?"

"Believe me I know."

"Wait, everyone's nearly off. I'm standing up."

Ahead of us a regimental line of people in dark-blue polos filed off a bus and started heading toward us down the walkway.

Sarah turned around. "Look, Mac. It's the Americans."

"Whaaaaat?! Wow! What are the odds of that!"

She raised an eyebrow and turned back around.

I grimaced. My 'mildly surprised' must have come off as 'shook to the core'. Maybe I should let Viv give me the acting lessons she'd been offering for the last eight years.

"Just getting off the bus now," Christine muttered.

She was framed in the bus doorway, her bag slung over her shoulder and her phone pressed to her ear.

My chest swelled. She stood on tiptoes then spotted me. My face and neck started to burn. Her attention fixed on me was like a bathroom ceiling heat lamp that could feel pleasant but would actually be searing after a long, hot shower.

She waited a few beats after the US team phalanx moved off and fell into step a couple of paces back. "So help me, how are you so sexy at the end of a travel day? I want my mouth all over you."

"Eep! Chrissie, you're not helping me out. I think I'm hyperventilating."

I lost sight of her as her team approached. Our squads were going to pass by each other in single file along the narrow walkway, cars parked in countless rows close to us on either side.

Her teammates started to file past me. There was a general hubbub of greetings and how are yous from both sides.

Finally I caught sight of Christine again. I could hear her breath through my phone. Ahead of me I saw Sarah nod at her, maybe say something, but Christine didn't even look at her. Her gaze was locked on me. Her lips were parted, and I was close enough to see she was gripping her phone tightly.

The heat intensified so much I was hurting. As she reached me, she flicked her eyes back over her shoulder for a split second then reached over and crumpled something small into my hand. Her fingers dragged for an agonising second along my palm. She exhaled again. I heard it in stereo through the phone and for real at the same moment.

Then her hand was gone from mine and she moved away. I turned around and started walking backwards. *Damn!* I had never seen a pair of navy-blue leggings worn so well.

She looked back at me over her shoulder and spoke softly. "I'm going to destroy you the next time I see you."

I gulped. "Same to you."

I walked backwards right into Sarah.

"Bloody hell! What is up with you today?"

I stretched my mouth out into a "my bad!" frown.

"Sounds like you better go," Christine said.

"Yeah."

"I'll call you tonight from Auckland. I wish I could wait for this plane curled up in a chair with you."

I panicked a little as tears pricked my eyes. "Right back at ya. Talk to you then! Bye now."

I stashed my bag in a pile with everyone else's and boarded the bus. I walked all the way to the back and sat by myself.

When the bus started to move, I unclenched my fist and unfolded the ripped vitamin water label I found there. Scribbled on the back were two words in blue biro.

I'm yours.

I let out a slow shuddering breath, leaned my head against the cool bus window and closed my eyes. I was filled with a deep longing. I wasn't used to this. I usually skimmed across the surface of life, worked hard and did my best, but never craved and strived, and never wanted like I did now. Not since college when my crush on Christine made me a little loopy. This was more intense though.

Did it feel good? The short answer was no. It felt like I was driving a car that was picking up speed down a hill toward the edge of a cliff.

I got an intense flashback from our night in Perth. Different city, different bus, but for a moment I was back there, gripping the back of her neck to pull her mouth toward mine and kissing her with complete abandon. That had felt good. So good that even thinking about it now made every nerve in my body thrum. I knew in that moment I would never get my fill of her. So where did that leave me?

I grabbed my phone.

I'm yours too.

Fletch lay gently snoring in the hotel bed next to mine. I couldn't sleep so was scrolling through my phone.

The US had beaten England the night before, which meant we would play each other in the must-win semi-final. I'd sent a text that morning:

Good game! I guess I know when I'm seeing you next ;)

No reply. I'd obsessed all day. Was the wink lame? Was the fact we were going to be opponents a major issue and I shouldn't be making a joke about it?

My eyes stung from staring at the images racing up my little screen as I flicked my thumb again and again. *I should turn in. Lie awake, but give my poor eyes a rest.*

My phone started to vibrate. Incoming call from Rose! I scrambled to get out of bed, my legs flailing. I didn't want to wake Fletch, but haste was vital. If I missed the call maybe Christine would put her phone straight to airplane mode and go to bed. I got my knee caught in the bedspread, tripped and fell so hard against Fletch's bed it slid half a metre across the carpet.

I froze.

They snuffled once then kept snoring. Maybe having heaps of siblings made a person a heavy sleeper. I sprinted to the door, grabbing a room key on the way.

I took a couple of big bounds away from the door. I couldn't wait for it to close before answering.

"Hello, hello! Yes?"

"Keeley?"

"Yes! Sorry, hi. I had to run out of the room because Fletch was asleep."

"Oh, yeah. Sorry it's so late. Coach kept the leadership group in a meeting for hours."

"Hah! So much for rest days, hey?"

"Totally."

A pause. "Yeah. So, uh, congrats on making it to the semi-finals. That's huge." I sat down cross-legged on the floor, my back against the wall. The carpet was thin—more like a layer of rigid felt than anything that was supposed to provide comfort. I looked up and down the hallway as I waited for her to respond.

They'd dimmed the lights, probably so guests wouldn't have a bright bar of light under the doors to their rooms while they were trying to sleep.

I shivered a little in the Brisbane Lions pjs Viv had gotten me for Christmas.

"Thanks. I'm looking forward to it. And to seeing you. But it will be kind of weird."

My shoulders relaxed a little. "Yes. Weird, all right."

"I've never played against someone I was, um, seeing, before."

I chuckled. "Seeing? Is that what the kids are calling it these days?"

She laughed too. "Sorry, that was kind of a dumb way to put it. Hey, don't be mad, but I won't be able to phone or text you the next couple of days until after the match. Coach has us on this ultimate focus mindframe thing. So much for rest days, huh?"

I got a twinge in my chest, but my brain jumped in to override it. I had been worried about my focus in the lead-up to the match too. This was good for me as well. A relief. A disappointing relief. "That's okay, Chrissie. I get it."

She sighed. "God, you're the best, you know that? I miss you."

"I miss you too. Um…" I bit my lip. The thought had popped into my head that I wondered if she would struggle being my direct opponent again for this next game. Maybe that's what her hours-long meeting had been about. After all, Christine had played poorly by her standards last time we'd gone head-to-head. And I knew that she *had* been thrown, seeing me again after so many years. It would be all kinds of wrong to even hint at these thoughts.

My stomach twisted. I liked things to be simple!

"Were you going to say something?" she asked.

"No, nothing. Just, I better let you get to bed."

"I guess so. I wish I was sleeping with you tonight and not Mikayla. I mean—you know what I mean! Separate beds, nothing shady."

I smiled. "All good, you dag. I know what you mean. Good night."

"Bye, Keeley. Good night." She hung up but I kept the phone next to my ear.

I tried to hold onto the image of her mouth right next to her phone, speaking softly to me. I leaned the back of my head against the wall. Every little bit of me, every atom, was exhausted. From the gruelling tournament schedule but also from longing, from wanting.

I sighed as I pulled my feet under me, hefted myself up and headed back in to an unconscious and oblivious Fletch.

Chapter 19

CHRISTINE GRIPPED MY HAND.

"Good luck," we both said at the exact same time. She patted my shoulder briskly—more of a tap, really—then she greeted the player behind me with the exact same tone.

I buzzed with electricity all over. From being close to Christine, from the energy from the sold-out Stadium Australia—the floodlights, the noise, the occasion—it all felt unreal. I stepped into position at right-back and tried to centre myself in the moment. But the moment was too noisy and too bright.

Christine positioned herself at the halfway line, upfield from me. We would be direct opponents again.

She had spent hours with her team and coaches figuring out ways to take me and my team down. The thought stung, even though my camp and I had done the same for her.

But even though it was irrational, I couldn't fight the feeling that there were two Christines—the one who kissed me gently and made my heart pound when she looked at me, and this international superstar who was my fierce rival.

I glanced at Ava, my fellow defender. Her nostrils were flared and she was staring fiery red hatred right at Christine. She wanted Christine to lose. Did I? I wanted to win. Was there a difference?

I shook my arms and jumped on the spot. There were dozens of women playing this tournament grappling with the same question. Women from all over the world flung together in the big English,

European and US domestic clubs, falling in love, and now playing in opposition as they represented their home countries. Hell, some couples played against each other week in, week out. If they made it work, why couldn't Christine and I?

The ref's whistle blew and we were on.

The US had possession, and it only took them four kicks to get the ball downfield toward their goal. Mikayla Larkin took the ball in the centre and looked for her best striker.

I ran toward Christine and reached her just as Mikayla's lofted pass hit her on the chest. She pressed her back against me, her weight and eyeline both going left like she was going to pass back into the middle. But I knew better. She was the smartest player I knew, and I'd seen her dozens of times at Florida State assess the most likely thing to do, then fool everyone and do the hard thing instead.

So then she twisted right, away from goal and away from her teammates expecting her pass, but I was ready for her. I went with her, step for step, just the two of us running toward the corner flag. I was too close to her. If she took her chance and went around me she would probably win. But I felt no fear. What would happen would happen, and the consequences, even if I made a mistake, weren't going to kill me.

I tackled, getting just enough purchase on the ball that it bobbled behind her. I was quicker to change direction and won the ball, sprinting down the sideline like I had a pack of wolves after me.

I shot a cross in to Allie, who trapped the ball but then kicked it right to the keeper. She held her head in her hands, shook her shoulders, then gave me a thumbs up as she ran back into position.

Momentum teetered back and forth between our two teams. The crowd noise was a constant roar, with strains of our cheer squad's drumming, chants and songs threaded through.

We forayed forward again. Fletch got on the outside and made a blinding run. Their shot was amazing, but the US goalie flung sideways and, horizontal at a full stretch, caught the ball in both gloves before it could cross the goal line.

She then threw a tantrum, flinging her arms around and shouting expletives at her defenders. They turned their backs on her and became fascinated with straightening their socks, shoelaces or headbands.

The goalie gave the ball an almighty kick, high and long. I lost sight of it in the lights, then got a jolt of adrenaline.

Shit!

I was the closest person on my team to where it was going to land. I sprinted forwards. A shape planted itself in my path. Christine.

She turned her back on me to face the falling ball. I stopped at her right shoulder. I felt rather than saw her head turn my way for the briefest moment.

I lunged backwards then launched myself toward the ball with everything I had. Christine rose beside me. But she didn't impact my jump, and I headed the ball with a flick of my neck and shoulders, out and safely over the sideline.

We landed with a thud and I overbalanced and went down on one knee. Fletch hoisted me up by my armpits, pounding me on the back and yelling incoherent congratulations and compliments right next to my ear.

I regained my balance, ready to find Christine and restart our battle after her throw-in.

But it was Summer Ryland picking up the idly bouncing ball, looking around for someone to toss it to. Christine was way over on the opposite side of the field, jogging to her position alongside Ava.

Never in any of the hours of tape of different games I had watched Christine play had she ever played on that wing. It was very weird, but I didn't have time to mull over it because Summer sent the ball flying into play and we were back on.

Half-time rolled around with no change to the 0-0 scoreline. In the rooms Ava crashed down on the bench next to me. She was an intense character and her years playing in Spain had made her even more so.

"What the fuck is Delacourt doing on my wing?"

"Whoa, slow your roll. How am I supposed to know?"

"Well, I've only studied Ryland and Barker. If the US is trying to fuck with my head, then, bravo, they've done it!" She slumped over and held her head with both hands.

I rubbed her back and smiled. She was one of the most elite sportswomen in the world, but at this moment she was no different from Viv working herself up over how many lyrics she had to learn for the Elwood Amateur Theatre Troupe's recent staging of *Hamilton.*

Coach strode up and leaned over so her face was close to mine. "Why is Delacourt playing left-field? She never plays left-field."

I threw my hands up and shook my head. "I have literally no idea. I don't know." It technically wasn't a lie. I didn't *know* why Christine had put as much distance as possible between her and me. But I had a sneaking suspicion.

Coach stood upright, closed her eyes and took a deep breath. "Okay, okay. You're right. How are you meant to know?" She made a gesture with both hands like she was parting the red sea.

Ava and I scooched so she could sit between us.

Coach leaned her head back against the wall.

I glanced past her at Ava, who gave a little shrug.

"Did you want me to, uh, switch sides to play on Christine?" I asked, managing with great effort to sound nonchalant. I balled both my fists on my knees.

"No, no, no. You are terrible at left-back whereas Ava is the best in the world at it."

Ava nodded. I would have been annoyed if both facts weren't so undeniable.

Coach sighed. "No, we can only hope Delacourt is as bad over that side as you, Keeley. Now, you have six minutes to tell us absolutely everything you know about her."

Of course I stuck to everything *soccer-related* I knew about Christine. Six minutes didn't allow me to divulge that she liked yellow Starburst but hated red. Or that she was ticklish across her belly—how even the slightest breath against her skin would bring up goosebumps and cause her to throw her head back and... *Get it together! Your national pride is on the line!*

Six minutes later I'd given Ava a crash course on Christine's playing style and it was time to take the field again. Christine lined up at the halfway line, inches from the Ava's sideline. I wondered what the sports journalists and commentators were making of Christine's unexpected switch. Ava had her eyes narrowed and was staring lasers right at her, muttering. Whether she was going over my information and committing it to memory or voicing physical threats of violence against Christine to gee herself up—I didn't know and I would never ask. Ava was a weirdo soccer genius and her process was her own.

I watched Christine, gently pressing the fingertip of each finger to her thumb, back and forth in a steady rhythm. She couldn't play on me. I shook her focus. Right now, did she regret ever developing feelings for me? Kissing me four years ago after what had been, back then, the greatest win of our lives?

And this new fling, which had consumed me since the start of the tournament. I was all in on Christine, and everything about her made my life better. But was she ever all in on me? Especially now, when she was struggling, with the eyes of the world on her?

76th minute, score 0-0

The US's Cam Barker received a perfect pass and ran toward me. The crowd noise kicked up a notch, making me think something was going on behind me. I wanted to look, but my job was Cam. She stopped her run dead. My weight was going backwards and she caught me off-guard. I sprinted toward her but couldn't get there before she fired a lofted pass over my head into the centre. I swung round.

Ava and Christine were neck and neck, our goalie was the only other player within cooee. I appealed for offside, yelling my head off at the sideline ref closest to me. No dice.

I watched Ava and Christine. I felt Cam come and stand next to me, just two more enthralled spectators of the play in front of us.

As soon as Christine's feet left the ground I knew. Her movements had the beauty of split-second precision timing. She soared above Ava to meet the ball at its highest point, and it flew off her head, past the goalie into the back of the net.

"Offside, offside!" Fletch and Ava appealed to the match referee.

"They've already checked the tape. She was good," she replied.

I stood to the side, watching Christine's teammates mob her and celebrate wildly. Then I turned my back on them and ran to my backline.

"We need to score to win," I said urgently. "It starts with us. On the front foot. Let's not go to bed tonight wondering if we tried hard enough. We can fucking do this!"

88th minute US 1—AUS 0

The impossible happened. US captain Summer Ryland mucked up a pass in the centre of the field and the ball bobbled into no man's land. Fletch pounced.

"Go, go, go, fucking go!" I screamed, running forward after them.

I don't know if my teammates heard me, but they saw me and started streaming toward goal with energy that was almost unbelievable so late in the game.

Fletch was confronted by two opponents and flicked the ball out sideways to me. All I knew was I had to keep it moving. The US hadn't had time set up their impenetrable defence. I didn't pick out a player, I just booted it forward and ran to follow it. The ball thumped off the goalie's shinguard and ricocheted back into a clump of players. Then, as if we were suddenly a hive-mind, we pressed forwards at once and almost through sheer force of will pushed the ball over the line into the goal.

Our celebration was enthusiastic but brief. I didn't even know then which of our players was awarded the goal. The US players were still remonstrating with the referee as we sprinted back and took our kick-off formation.

"We've got the momentum! Let's do this" I screamed at Fletch. They nodded as if they heard me, but I couldn't even hear myself.

Straight after the US kicked off again the assistant referee held up the board announcing two minutes had been added to make up for injury time.

The crowd noise was deafening. It sounded like one big, long yell. Mikayla Larkin for the US made a bustling run up the centre. It looked like she was going to try and win it off her own boot.

But then she seemed to change her mind and turned her shoulder away from the goal and swung a long-range pass backwards. The defender was on the back foot, a split second slow to come and meet it. Our captain Allie jumped like a jack rabbit and ran like the clappers to steal the ball.

Allie caressed the ball into the goal like her boot was sending the net a love letter. The goalie had no chance of stopping the course of true love.

Allie fell to her knees and gave a roar of excitement, then quickly jumped to her feet, lifted her arm and pointed back to the centre of the field. We had a 2-1 lead, but the game wasn't over yet.

The US kicked off shallow and Summer Ryland took possession. Ava and Allie shut her down immediately and tackled the ball over the sideline. Just as the sideline ref's flag went up, the head referee blew three long blasts of her whistle.

We'd won. We'd actually freaking won.

Every member of the US team fell to the ground at once as if struck down by an invisible laser beam.

I turned in a slow circle. The crowd noise seemed like it was reaching me from a long way underwater. A guy in the stands had taken off his gold jersey and was waving it around his head like a helicopter blade. Wasn't he cold, bare-chested in the middle of the night?

Fletch crashed into me so hard I fell to the ground. They sat on top of me and shook me by the collar.

I scrunched up my face. *Ow, quit it.*

"*We're into the final!* You and me, mate, we're going to play in a freaking World Cup goddamn final!"

The crowd noise came rushing back. My entire body jolted with adrenaline. We had pulled it off. Beaten the US to give ourselves a chance of winning the whole thing.

"Shit," I said. I pushed Fletch off me and jumped up. I kept jumping up and down on the spot, waving my arms around like a mad thing. I picked out my shirtless friend in the crowd and yelled right to him. "We won, we won, we won!"

He started jumping in time with me, beaming from ear to ear.

I turned and ran. I needed to hug every single one of my teammates and tell them the news. *We won!*

I pulled up short as I nearly crashed into someone. US player Mikayla Larkin was crouched on her haunches with her head bowed.

Oh. I scanned the pitch. Christine stood unmoving. With her arms by her sides the way she was holding herself could have been mistaken for an easy stance. Except for her face. The intensity as she looked unseeing into the middle distance was frightening. I could almost feel the disappointment and desolation as they raged through her like storm systems.

I wanted to take her in my arms and cradle her head against my shoulder so badly that my fingers twitched.

A cameraperson ran straight up and trained their lens right at her.

She didn't acknowledge it. Nothing from the outside was getting in.

The possibility of holding her and providing her comfort blew away like firework smoke.

One of the US support staff came over and hugged her. She slung her arms around his waist in return and hid her nose and mouth against his shoulder. He walked off and she went to follow him. I jogged a few steps to catch up with her.

"Christine!" I called.

She turned. She tensed as I approached, her forehead creasing into a frown. She grasped my hand in a business-like shake.

"Seems like no matter what I do, when it comes to you, I can't win," she said.

"I…" I snapped my mouth shut. *I'm sorry?* I wasn't sorry we'd won, but I was sad that she was disappointed. "Can I call you tomorrow?"

She took a slow measured breath in through her nose.

Gravity tripled, and my knees had to work hard to keep me upright. My stomach felt like lead.

"Yes," she said.

Gravity went back to normal but my heart still beat fast. "Okay," I replied.

She nodded once then took her hand from mine and walked away.

The dial tone buzzed and buzzed in my ear. I shielded my eyes from the sunlight bouncing off the water. Just when I was going to give up and hang up I heard her voice.

"Hey," she said.

"Chrissie."

I paused, trying to think of what to say next. *I've been calling and calling. I thought you might have lost your phone?*

"Congratulations on the win. You played well," she said.

"Um, thanks. Are you in Brisbane yet?"

The US and China were playing off for third place in two days' time. We'd meet Canada in the final the day after.

"Yeah, we arrived this morning. How's Sydney?"

"Yeah good. Spectacular, actually. I'm, well, I wanted to get out by myself, so I've come to Circular Quay."

I took in the iconic Sydney Harbour view again. The imposing arc of the Harbour Bridge to my left, the Opera House to my left, all lit and glamourised by impossibly blue sparkling water. There was a reason this scene was recreated on countless mugs, tea towels and fridge magnets—it was beautiful.

She gave a tiny chuckle, barely more than a hiss. "The total tourist experience. Are you hoping to be recognised by all the folks in town for the final? Get mobbed by fans?"

I crinkled my nose. Her tone was pretty light. I usually loved it when she teased me. But I thought underneath there was a shred of bitterness in her voice.

I blew on past it. "Something like that. I've got a baseball cap pulled low and big sunglasses. I'm channelling Britney Spears on an In-N-Out run. Hey, um, how are you going…with everything?"

Silence.

"Christine?"

"Yah, I'm here. I can't talk long. Our tournament's not done. We still gotta train."

"Yes, I know that, I—can I call you tonight?"

A pause, but not silence. A long breath, then, "I don't think so. My team needs me. They see me as a leader, an example. I've got to be all in on this third-place play-off match, or else the newer girls might think there's nothing to play for. I've got to put them first."

Panic rose in my chest. This was a rejection. The picture-perfect day I was looking at was blighted by imaginary storm clouds rolling in from both sides. I gripped the edge of the big stone step I was sitting on. *Breathe.*

She was rejecting my offer to phone her later, not *me* in my entirety. It was like watching a ball sail in from long-range. You have to choose whether to jump on it aggressively and send it back with more heat on it, or cradle it gently down to the ground with your boot and look after it lovingly for a bit while you assess your options.

I chose the latter. "Hey, totally, no worries at all. Take as much time as you need. I'll, uh, probably see you at the FIFA awards thing, on Monday night?" I was playing it cool, but I'd asked our team publicist Brianna whether the third and fourth-placed teams would be invited to the awards ceremony in Sydney after all the matches were finished.

She had said they would be, as well as the captains and outstanding performers from all the other teams.

"Yes, we'll be going along," Christine replied.

"Oh, awesome. It's going to be pretty ritzy, by all accounts. Should be fun."

"Yeah. They had all our formalwear shipped to the venue weeks ago."

"Oh shit, that's smart. I'm going to have to scramble and find something after the game."

She chuckled properly this time. "You mean to tell me, the day after you play in the final of the World Cup, you're going to be schlepping around Sydney by yourself looking for a suit?" The warmth had returned to her voice.

I could tell she was smiling. A shaft of sunlight parted my storm clouds.

"Not by myself. I helped Fletch pack and I know they don't have anything either. Hey, and how do you know I'll pick a suit? I was thinking of asking a seamstress to recreate one of Sarah Jessica Parker's looks from the Met Gala."

"Hah! You *have* to pair the dress with those gloves that go up higher than your elbows. Or I'm sure there's some fancy butchers in town. Why don't you go for Lady Gaga's meat dress?"

"Brilliant idea. You bring the tomato sauce and we can throw a barbeque for the after-party."

"Yum. You know I can't eat rump steak unless it's been sat on for an entire three-hour awards ceremony. I always did like you in a suit though." The warmth-o-meter had cranked up another notch with that last sentence.

I grinned. "All right, I'll cancel the beef. You're more important than high fashion."

"I'll see ya, Keeley. I've gotta run now though."

"All good. Can I text you before Monday?"

"Of course you can text me. Good luck in your match."

"You too. China are tough, but I think you got them. If you put them off their possession game with intense forward pressure they can crack."

"You sound like Coach in our meeting this morning. Thanks. I'll see ya."

"Yeah, see ya."

The Manly ferry pulled out from the Quay, sending a couple of pelicans flapping off to one of the islands. My insides were like the churn behind the big boat.

Were we good? Were we not? When I dialled the phone I half thought I would be brave enough to casually mention that the World Cup would be over in a few days. Her big barrier to even turning her mind to the future—to our future—was about to be removed.

We'd been doing a beautiful aerial circus act together for the past few weeks. And shit it had been fun. And thrilling. Completely captivating. But now the net was about to be whisked out from under us.

Ker-splat!

Pelican shit hit the pathway at the water's edge, narrowly missing a tour group in matching white T-shirts and red, wide-brimmed hats. They shrieked and scrambled, then gasped laughingly once they'd checked they weren't covered in poo. A few of the onlookers sharing the big stone steps with me chuckled along.

Not me. My wrists ached and I let go of the edge of the step I'd been gripping with both hands. Christine had pulled back from me slightly—with a justifiable reason and no promises broken—but my sunshine had been taken away. There was a good chance when I saw her next that she'd tell me she might be done with me for good.

I hugged both arms across my belly and hung my head.

Chapter 20

My brain was buzzing and it was hard to focus on anything, especially under the big TV lights. Because, hello, Australia had won the goddamn actual World Cup! Bloody hell! Nope, I was never ever going to get tired of that thought. But holy moley it was hard to climb down off the adrenaline high.

"I'm sorry, Lisa, could you please repeat that? Just, sorry—" I held the microphone with its big foam cover away from my mouth and shielded my eyes from the white lights. "Oi, can it, Ava! I'm live on telly!"

From behind the camera operator her silhouette flipped me the double bird to the uproarious amusement of a few of my teammates who were milling around.

Brianna shooed them out of my eyeline. The team had taken over one of the hotel function rooms for various press and publicity spots. Fletch was somewhere on their phone doing an interview with the ABC. I was live via satellite on breakfast TV in Melbourne.

I looked back down the lens with what I hoped was a winning smile. "High spirits here, Lisa. I apologise."

I heard laughter through the earpiece, then a tinny voice said, "No problem. Perfectly understandable given last night's amazing win! Now, can you talk us through the last ten minutes of the match? The Canadians just kept on coming for you."

"They sure did, Lisa. After Allie's header put us one goal up, it was tempting to go into our shells to try to maintain the lead. But Fletch and Ava and I knew we couldn't play keepings off for ten full minutes plus extra time. Full credit to the Canadian team—they were super competitive and left it all out on the park. Whenever we got the ball back we tried to create something—make them defend.

"Those last minutes, and then injury time, flew by because we weren't watching the clock. I didn't hear the final whistle because the crowd was so loud, but Fletch and Sarah just jumped literally on top of me—completely knocked me over, then I knew we'd won."

"Just amazing. And what does the win mean to you?"

"It means so much. I mean, Australia's been playing in the World Cup since 1995 when only twelve teams were in it. This year thirty-two countries played, and this is the first time we've won it." I paused. "To achieve this, with this group of teammates, in front of the biggest crowd that's ever watched a women's sporting match ever—it's everything." Tears pricked the back of my eyes.

"Keeley, it's Tony here. Which special people were in that huge crowd, cheering you on?"

My breath caught and my throat swelled. "I was lucky enough to have my mum and dad there—aw jeez." As I'd been dreading, my voice came out thick with emotion. "You're making me tear up. Sorry. They just left for the airport a few minutes ago. And my best friend and housemate Viv was there. She means the world to me as well."

"It's Lisa here again, Keeley. I just have one last question—how hard are you and the team going to party for the next few days now that you're the world champs?"

I laughed. "Oh, well, we cut loose a bit last night—I haven't actually slept, so, hah, that might give you some indication. And we've got the FIFA awards tonight which a lot of players from other teams are going to, so that will be good."

"Keeley, I know your whole camp is in celebration mode, but will you have any feeling of, I don't know…sadness, that the tournament is done? It must have been such a rollercoaster to share this experience. Is there anyone you'll be sorry to say good-bye to now life is returning to normal."

"Uhhhhh…" *Christine.* I blinked a few times rapidly. *The electricity I felt when she touched me after that first match.* I could feel my face going bright red. *Her mouth on mine as I pushed her against the side of the bus.* I cleared my throat. "Um, yes! Of course. My Matildas teammates have all become like family. And I have to give a shout out to our incredible coaching and support staff. We wouldn't win any trophies without them."

"Well, thanks for your time today, Keeley. Here in the studio we're all decked out in our green and gold to celebrate your historic win. Congratulations again. And, uh, try to stay away from any dumpsters between now and your big party tonight."

"Yep, Tony, thanks for that, I'll try. Thanks so much!"

I stood frozen grinning down the camera lens. My insides still quivered. I took a deep breath but it didn't help. I had no control over the force of my feelings.

The big square light shut off and the camera operator stepped forward. "We got it. My producer says they've moved onto a segment about whether you should use egg whites as night cream."

"Oh, right. Thanks."

She started breaking down the light tripod.

Brianna took the chunky battery pack off the back of my pants waistband and reached under my polo shirt to tear off the tape fixing the cord to my belly.

"Well done, Keels. You were just a tad shaky, though. Very unlike you. I'll get the station to e-mail me the broadcast, and we can go through it if you want? You'll have a few more interviews through an earpiece at the awards tonight."

"Oh, nah, I'm right thanks Bree. I think I'm just tired. I only caught a few minutes' sleep top to toe with Fletch in the bathtub in Allie's room."

She rolled her eyes. "Right, well. Try to catch a couple of hours today if you can."

"I'll try. Fletch and I have to go buy outfits for tonight at some stage though."

She dropped both arms to her sides, her eyes wide. "You were meant to have something sorted before the tournament began. Do either of you even read my e-mails?"

"Errrrrr. Well, I don't see why we're expected to lug fancy clothes from city to city for weeks. The US team got theirs shipped straight to the venue."

"Well, I'm sorry, your royal highness. Ava has been 'lugging' a gold lamé cocktail dress from city to city without complaints and without a single crease! How do you know that about the Americans anyway?"

I shrugged. "Uh, I dunno. People talk."

The camera operator walked over. *Oh thank you, Mother Universe!*

"We're all packed up. Thanks again for arranging this, Brianna. Mac, I've gotta say, I'm a huge fan. The Matildas have made us all proud."

"Aw, thanks Jodie," I said.

Brianna's eyes flicked to mine.

Yeah, I took note when she introduced herself, like a super-professional. "That means a lot. Hey, did they let you know how that other segment went? I generally make pavlova out of all my leftover egg whites, but I'm open to suggestions."

She laughed and went a bit pink. Nice smile. Long dark hair and a checked flannel under a jacket. Usually a style I stopped to take a second look at.

"Turns out the cream stops wrinkles but makes your skin smell so bad that nobody wants to go near you," she said.

"Hah! A classic catch-22."

"Something like that. Hey, I better make tracks."

"Sure thing, Jodie. Thanks again."

She gave another nice smile and an awkward wave.

I turned to Brianna and raised my eyebrows.

She narrowed her eyes. "Are you done flirting?"

"I wasn't *flirting,* I was *charming* an important member of the broadcast press. Just as I shall *charm* everyone tonight at the ball, *darling!*" I walked backwards toward the door, flourishing my arms.

"Hold on," she said loudly as I retreated. "Are you and Fletch going clothes shopping by yourselves?"

"No, pet. Don't be droll. Viv's taking us."

She slumped with visible relief. "Well thank fuck for small mercies!"

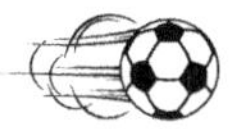

Our Uber driver Akmal dropped us off on a trendy street full of little boutiques in Bondi Junction. He was a soccer fan and was chuffed to be driving us.

"Aussie, Aussie, Aussie!" he called out the window as he pulled away from the curb.

"Oi oi oi!" Fletch and I replied, waving.

"Five stars for that nice gentleman," Viv said, tapping her phone.

"We gonna walk to the Westfield shopping centre from here?" asked Fletch.

"West—*Westfield*?" Viv spluttered. "I am not letting you two wear off-the-rack tonight! Would you wear off-the-rack department store outfits to the Tony Awards?"

Fletch looked sideways at me and I looked sideways at them.

"Ummmmm..." Fletch played for time.

Viv had her arms crossed and one eyebrow raised.

I took a stab. "No?"

"Exactly! Tonight is football's night of nights, and the two most important people in my life are going to look the part."

She threw an arm around each one of us and steered us into a tiny shop with polished wood floors and old-looking plasterwork all over the ceiling. Dozens and dozens of suits lined the racks on each side of the room.

"You must be Vivienne!" A woman with grey curly hair piled on top of her head and a tape measure looped around her neck stood up from a stool next to the back counter and threw her arms wide. "Come through, come through. Let me show you what I've been working on."

"Working on?" I muttered to Fletch as Viv greeted the woman and we trooped through a narrow door to a back room.

The woman flicked on a light and two headless dressmakers' dummies appeared in front of us. One was dressed in a dark grey suit, with a single-breasted jacket with one row of lighter grey buttons. The other wore a suit of deep midnight blue. The jacket crossed over and was fastened by two sets of gold buttons. Both suits were so beautiful that Fletch and I said "Wow!" in unison and walked with our hands outstretched to touch the fabric. I took the sleeve of the blue suit and ran my thumb over the cuff.

I turned to Viv. "I don't know shit about this stuff, but this is the best-sewn suit I've ever seen."

Fletch was stroking the grey jacket. "Bloody nice," they said.

The woman smiled. "That's the type of reaction we're always after. Now, you'd better try them on to see if I've gotten Vivienne's instructions right."

Viv giggled. "Don't look so stunned. Keeley—when you told me about needing an outfit for this gala, I reached out to some theatre people I knew up here. Everyone said the *only* place to get a suit made in Sydney was at Fiona's boutique. She's retired from making stage costumes now, but is still the best tailor in the state. I sent her your measurements and what I thought you might like the suit to look like, and here we are."

I threw my arms around her then held her shoulders at arms' length. "You are the absolute best, you know that? One question though, how do you have my measurements?"

"Oh, I just made my best guesstimate. You sew enough costumes for community theatre troupes, you get a feel for that type of thing."

Fiona nodded.

Viv put her hand on Fletch's shoulder. "I just hope I've done justice to your lovely long legs, Fletch. Try it on, the suspense is killing me!"

Fletch looked at Viv's hand on their shoulder and blinked hard.

"Come on," I said.

Fiona started undressing both the dummies. Viv took us back into the shop and rifled through a rack of white button-up shirts before grabbing a hanger with a flourish.

She held the shirt against Fletch's front and draped two undone bowties over their shoulder. She narrowed her eyes then shook her head and grabbed a bright blue one.

"Perfect," she said. "It will bring out your eyes."

Fiona came in with the suits. "Be very careful, the cuffs are only pinned! I've eyeballed it and Vivienne seems to have got your measurements spot on. You're a natural dear." She patted Viv's cheek, spun us around and pushed us toward two curtained cubicles at the back of the shop.

"I don't know how I feel about all these women eyeballing my anatomy," I said.

"I have a feeling you love it, dear. Now go on!" She pulled the curtain shut behind me.

"Do I get a shirt?" I asked.

"No shirt," Fiona and Viv replied.

"Huh?" I dropped my shorts.

"The jacket's designed to be worn by itself. Don't worry, the inside panelling won't rub," said Fiona.

"I thought you might want to show off some decolletage tonight, Keels. You know, special occasion and all that?"

I held my T-shirt collar out and peered down. "Are we sure that's a good idea? I mean, I like what I'm working with, but I'm not sure my assets will do the outfit justice."

"Trust me, you'll look great. This is the '20s, baby! Flat is in, just like it was 100 years ago."

I frowned into the mirror. "Flat is in…" I muttered to myself as I pulled the jacket on. Then louder, "I can see my bra above where the jacket, you know, criss-crosses."

"No bra!" Fiona and Viv said in unison.

My face in the mirror was scandalised. "No way! What if I have, you know, a slip?"

Viv poked her head through the curtain. "Quit being such a baby. I'll do you up with so much double-sided tape it'll take you an hour to get undressed. Unless you have someone helping you of course." She batted her eyelashes.

My stomach dipped. The hours were passing slow but also incredibly fast until I would see Christine again. I was trying not to think about it. I rolled my eyes and gave Viv a little push. "Shoo, creeper. I gotta take off my bra *apparently*."

"Ready?" asked Fletch from the next cubicle a minute later.

"Yep. Three, two, one."

We pulled our curtains aside and strode barefoot into the shop. Viv squealed and jumped up and down clapping her hands. Fiona said "yes" and bustled up to me and tugged my sleeves.

I looked over at Fletch. They had their shirt buttoned all the way up to the top and their bowtie hanging down from each side of their collar. Their face shone as Viv took up both ends and began to tie it nimbly.

"I became an expert at this when we took *The Importance of Being Earnest* on the road. We played every midsized house in the Pacific North-West." She looked up into Fletch's face and smiled, patting the completed bow. "Absolutely perfect."

Fletch did look amazing. The suit fit like a glove, and I had never realised how long their legs were.

"And what am I, chopped liver?" I asked.

They both turned and blinked at me like they'd forgotten I was there.

"You look great Mac," said Fletch.

Fiona ran her hand along the seam at my exposed breastbone.

"Geez, Fiona. Buy a girl a drink first," I said.

She scoffed, then stepped back and appraised me. "I won't need to do any alterations. You did well, Vivienne. I'll only need to adjust the pant cuffs depending on what you're going to do for shoes."

"Shoes?" I looked around. "Do you sell shoes, Fiona?"

"I don't, but there's a Westfield three blocks away where you can pick some up."

"That's a good idea," said Viv.

"Buy some shoes… off the *rack!* Not from an artisan vegan leatherworker who gets visited by fair trade *elves* in the *night*?"

Viv pursed her lips and turned to Fiona. "I would like to tell you that becoming a world champion has made her like this, but the truth is she's always been impossible."

Fiona had a dozen pins pressed between her lips, so she just grunted.

Viv filled Fiona in on the shoes we would both wear and we arranged to pick up our completed suits later on.

We both thanked Fiona profusely. She waved us away saying, "I hope they're paying you some decent prize money for last night. I've been called many things in my long life, but I've never been called cheap!"

Chapter 21

Viv arrived at our hotel suite with two theatre associates who had come to do Fletch's and my hair and make-up. Fletch went very minimal with the make-up, and they looked dashing with their hair swept back elegantly.

The team was putting us up in nicer rooms than usual in the hotel where the awards ceremony was being held.

I'd gone for more make-up, and my hair was artfully ruffled. I was amazed how much product it took to make me look like I'd slept in some shrubbery, but sneaking a look at myself reflected in the glass doors, I had to admit I didn't look half bad.

"Admiring yourself?" Viv asked, leaning back on the couch. Her glam crew had left a little while ago and Fletch and I were killing time before we had to go down and do a step and repeat in the foyer so people could take our photos.

"Your friends are true artists, mate," I sat down next to her. "I can't thank you enough for today. It's all been like a queer *Pretty Woman* fantasy. You constantly amaze me, but I know I shouldn't be surprised. You're a legend." I pulled her into a hug. "I love you," I said, my mouth pressed against her soft blonde head.

"Aw, I love you too. I had the best fun. It was my queer *Pretty Woman* fantasy to go on a massive spending spree on your dime, Richard Gere."

We leaned back on the couch and I took her hand.

"Hey, uh, Fletchy," she said. "I hate to ask, but could you please give us a second?"

"Okay, sure thing. Take as long as you need," they said, sliding open the glass door and stepping out onto the balcony. They grasped the railing and looked out over the city.

Viv now clasped both my hands and turned so our knees were touching.

I sat up a bit straighter.

She cleared her throat. "I just want to take this opportunity to say…" she paused.

"Jeez, spit it out. You've got me nervous."

She took a deep breath. "Tonight, with Christine, I don't want you to half-ass it."

"Half-arse it?"

"Half-ass it," she said, nodding. "Look, I see the focus and dedication you give to soccer. Extra training, studying the game 'til all hours of the morning, going jogging even when it's sleeting outside—you're all in. But, when it comes to women, you just kind of, you know, slide over the surface. Easy come, easy go." She tilted her head and appraised me with her massive blue eyes.

A quip sprang to mind—*easy come? You've been talking to my last three dates!*—but I bit it back. I owed it to her to listen properly.

I sighed and squeezed her fingers. "I guess, if I work hard at soccer I get more and more control over what happens in a game. But with relationships you never have control, so what's the point of working?"

She brushed my cheek with her fingertips. "I hear you, Keels, I do. And I normally wouldn't say to any 25-year-old woman that they have to buckle down and partner off. That 'twin flames' soulmate shit is half patriarchy, half capitalism trying to keep us unhappy so we buy stuff."

"Look, I know I'm a little dense, but this seems like mixed messages to me."

She grasped both my hands again. "Here's what I want to say. I can't tell you what you want. I can't tell you what's right for you. Just promise me you won't fuck yourself over because your default setting is laidback, easygoing rake. Do you want Christine?"

"Yes." The word was out of my mouth before I knew anything about it. But as I said it I knew it was true. Both joy and fear flooded through me from the tips of my toes to the top of my head.

I pulled Viv into a hug. "I promise I'll try."

"I'm proud of you. Now," she stood and held me at arms' length. "You'd better get to your party. How are you feeling?"

"Shaky and jittery and nervous and ill. If I didn't care about Christine, I would feel carefree and happy. I'm starting to think maybe you give terrible advice."

She held my face in both her hands. "Nerves are the performance enhancing drugs of the theatre world. You're going to be brilliant!" She spun me round and gave me a push, then rapped on the glass door to call Fletch back inside. "Depending on what happens, maybe we can get breakfast together tomorrow. My room's right next door."

"I'd like that," said Fletch.

"Good, now, you both look ravishing, you're the champions of the freaking world—go out there and do me proud. Break a leg!"

I was distracted during the step and repeat. They hadn't rolled out a red carpet, but photographers and journalists were lined up to take our photos with the tournament sponsors' logos on a long screen in the background. Fletch and I were among the first to arrive.

"Who are you wearing tonight?" a woman with an English accent and a TV camera next to her asked us.

"Uhhhhh…" Fletch and I looked at each other.

"Fiona?" they replied.

"I'm sorry," I said. "Could we come back in about a minute and have you ask us the same question again?"

"Well, we're actually live to thirty-six countries at the moment, so not really."

We moved on, but after a five-second phone call to Viv, we ran back up to the English journalist who was now interviewing the captain of the Dutch team. Fletch and I jostled into the frame.

"Uh, sorry to interrupt," I said. We're wearing Fiona Keats. Her shop Tailored For You is on Bronte Road in Bondi Junction. Suits for all genders! Thank you, good-bye."

I took Fletch's arm and walked back toward the entrance. "Let's watch people arrive."

"Yeah, okay, that could be cool," they said unenthusiastically. "Oh, hang about, I see Freya I used to play with at Hjørring. Back in two shakes."

I reached the entrance and waited for Christine. No phone to distract me, no quick chats with acquaintances passing by. I planted my feet and stared at the big foyer doors.

People arrived in dribs and drabs, but then there was a marked increase in the general hustle and bustle. The US team came into view en masse.

Shit they were cool. I didn't know how, but when they went somewhere as a group, they always seemed to be walking in slow motion. Especially today. Not one of them was smiling. Not many teams in the world would be disappointed with third place, but the US set unapologetically high standards for themselves.

I craned my neck. There! Near the back of the group. The team passed by me. I met Christine's eyes and she peeled off from the rest of her teammates.

My breath caught in my throat. She was wearing an emerald green cocktail dress, understated and stylish. Her shoulders were bare and she wore towering black high heels.

She stopped in front of me. "Hi," she said.

I swallowed but it didn't really work so I gulped loudly. "Sorry. You look amazing. You're so tall!"

"Don't be sorry," she said, smiling. "You look great too. Yeah, these shoes are a lot, hey?"

I gripped the bottom of my jacket with both hands. The urge to press my lips to her cheek, to find her mouth with mine, hit so hard it was painful.

I searched her face. Her eyes slid away from mine, down, down to where half a roll of double-sided tape allowed more than a slight hint of side-boob to show. Her lips parted and she took a light grasp of the fabric at the front of her skirt.

Her eyes found mine again. We stood there looking at each other in silence. The moment stretched out.

"Christine! They want a group photo," someone yelled. She blinked like she was being woken from a trance and swung her head around. "Coming," she called. Then, "Can we talk later?" she asked me quietly.

"Yes, I'll come find you in the break." I had made Brianna bring up the ceremony run sheet on her iPad and memorised it. They were giving us a forty-five-minute break in the proceedings to eat dinner.

Christine nodded and walked off.

The first half of the ceremony dragged. Endless speeches—the head of FIFA, the CEO of the car company that sponsored the tournament, and the COO of the sports brand sponsoring the awards.

They had us seated at big round tables with white tablecloths. Waitstaff brought around trays of champagne and beer, and the nine teammates I was sharing the table with were partaking liberally. I nursed a soda water and lime. I didn't want any booze putting me off my game (making me accidentally half-arse something I should devote my full arse to), and even caffeine was off the cards. My heart was already pattering—it didn't need any more stimulation.

The tables allocated to the US team were on the opposite side of the room and I sat with my back to them. I'd asked to swap with Allie on the other side of the table so I could have Christine in my eyeline, but Brianna saw us moving and ran over to say we had to stay in our assigned seats because the broadcast producers and camera people needed to be able to find us.

"What if either of you win the Golden Ball award? They need the reaction shot for the news. Doesn't anyone read my e-mails?"

The Golden Ball was the award for top player of the tournament. No Aussie had ever won it, but I hoped one of my teammates would get it tonight. They never gave it to defenders, so Fletch and I didn't have any expectations of our names being called.

Finally the break came. I jumped up and wove between the tables and chairs and the crush of people stretching their legs or looking around for the sign for the loos.

There was a flash of deep green in the corner of my eye and I wheeled around. Christine was pushing through the crowd toward the Australian tables.

"Christine!" I raised my arm. She heard me and changed direction. We stood close together. Encircled by a wall of people we had a degree of privacy.

"I'm staying here at the hotel. Did you want to come up to my room?" I asked.

Her eyes widened.

I winced. There was no way around how much that sounded like a blatant proposition.

"Yeah, let's go," she said.

We shared the lift with an older couple done up in very fancy clothes holding hands. We stood there next to them in silence. Once we were on the right floor, I led the way down the corridor to our room. I glanced sideways at Christine, remembering a similar charged atmosphere the night we'd walked down a hotel corridor after winning the NCAA championship. That night in the room she'd kissed me. I had no idea what would happen this time.

I unlocked the door and went in ahead of her, turning on the lights in the big living area. The door clicked shut behind us and her footsteps came toward me.

She stood next to me, both of us looking out toward the view beyond the balcony.

"It's not fair, you know," she said. "It's not fair, you looking this good tonight. I mean, you always look good, but tonight, you still look like you, but even more amazing. Breathtaking."

I felt like someone had poured a bottle of ice water down my back. "Why not fair?" I asked, keeping my tone steady.

She took a deep breath. It shook a little. "Because it makes this even harder. I think this has to be good-bye. I've thought it through every which way. When we get home I have to pivot to finishing off the NWSL season strong. Then Olympic selection. If this isn't the end for us, then what? I can't commit to long-distance, I can't commit to waiting and seeing and wondering—when there's no way this could end up good. No way. You mean too much to me to be a loose end that I have no chance of tying up. Do you see?"

I was stung. Anger and sadness welled up in my throat. She had made the decision to leave me behind. Again. Hurt spun around like a whirlpool in my stomach, threatening to suck me in. I wanted to fling cold words at her and walk out. If she didn't want me, then I would sure as hell show her that I didn't want or need her either.

My eyes rested on the couch in front of us. The memory of Viv squeezing my face in her hands rose in my mind. She had made me promise to fight for what I wanted. I stared past the couch to mine and Christine's reflection in the glass doors. Standing side by side looking serious like a couple in an olden days portrait.

With an extreme force of effort I tried to still the whirlpool. Only a sociopath would have been able to completely master their emotions in this situation, but I was able to calm down a little. *Fuck it!* I'd been in tight spots in soccer matches before. When every muscle cried out for rest and I was mentally exhausted. In those moments I always kept going. I didn't always win, but I kept going.

I stepped in front of her, right into her eyeline. She had clear access to the door behind her. She could leave if she wanted to. It was my job to make sure she didn't want to.

"Do you want me?" I asked. I stood up straight. I knew I looked fine as hell in my new suit, the curves of my breasts out there for all to see. She'd admired them before. They were hers to lose.

She looked into my face and her eyes creased in distress.

"If you don't want me, you don't want me. There's nothing I can do about that. But if you do want me, and you're afraid it's going to be hard, then hear me out."

Her jaw clenched. Her chest started to rise and fall. She didn't answer me.

"Because I want you. There's nothing I've even been so sure of in my whole life, and I've led a pretty simple, straightforward life with big dreams and clear goals. What we have—this attraction, this—what is it?—pull; you can't tell me it doesn't mean something.

"And it's not even just the sex. The pull is just as strong, like a force between my middle and yours. I go wild when my phone rings and it's you and maybe we'll get to talk to each other for two hours. Or when I picture us sitting on the couch deciding whether to watch *A League of Their Own* or *Orange is the New Black.* Or walking down the street together holding hands."

She pressed both her hands to her belly, spreading her fingers wide.

"You're the most driven person I know," I said. "For real. I'm a fighter too. Let's give this a shot. At least give ourselves a chance. I could come and play in the States, to be closer. Even if it's not the same city we could at least be in the same timezone. I'll do anything."

Her mouth started to crumple and she held her head to the side like her thoughts were too heavy to hold upright.

"Chrissie, please. I won't be able to deal if I can never touch you again. Never kiss you ever again." The truth of these words hit me hard and my voice got caught up in a sob. "You can't tell me you'd be okay with that. Please. Let's not go back to the party. Let's stay here, and say that we can be together, and I don't have to lose you again." The tears came and I couldn't speak any more. I reached forward but stopped before I grasped her hands.

She took a shuddering breath in. Her eyes slid away from mine and a tear rolled down her cheek. "I'm sorry, Keeley. I'm so sorry. I can't be your person. I can't." She turned and hurried away from me, fumbling with the door before rushing through it.

As it closed behind her I crouched down and hugged my knees, weeping huge racking sobs.

I crawled to the coffee table, grabbed my phone and called Viv.

Chapter 22

There was a gentle tap on the door.

"Tell them to go away," I said, snuffling and rubbing my nose with the back of my hand.

"Okay," said Viv gently.

I was curled up on the couch with my head resting against her chest. Her red *Rocky Horror Picture Show* cast T-shirt had a big wet patch in the middle where I'd cried on her. She unwound her arms and shifted little by little, moving my weight by degrees so I leaned against the back of the couch instead of her. She stood up and tiptoed away like she was leaving a ward full of sleeping sick people, or the bedroom of a toddler who was resting after a major meltdown.

"Is she in here?" Fletch asked.

Viv shooshed them. There was whispering then the padding of gentle footfalls.

"Hey, mate," said Fletch, crouching down and putting their hand on my shoulder. "The ceremony's done. Ava won the Golden Ball. We're taking a little break, then getting heaps of photos as a team in our nice clobber. Viv says you're not sick. What's the matter?"

I didn't move. "I want Christine Delacourt to be my girlfriend but she doesn't love me back," I said. It came out muffled because my chin was pressed hard into my chest. I felt heavy all the way through. Getting up off the couch was not going to be an option.

"Oh, uh, Christine Delacourt, you say? I see, I see." They patted my shoulder again and stood up, then said to Viv in a whisper that an audience would have been able to hear in the back row. "This happened to my uncle a few years ago. Complete nervous breakdown. He had a delusion he was engaged to Jennifer Lopez."

"No, Fletch," Viv said in a non-whisper. "Keeley has been seeing Christine. They dated in college and got back in contact during the tournament." She sat down next to me and hefted my curled-up form back onto her chest, putting her arms around me tight. "She's been so brave, and told Christine she wants them to be together. But… well—she said it herself—Christine doesn't feel the same way."

I sniffled, the tears threatening to return. "I don't feel brave, I feel stupid," I said.

"Hey, now," said Viv, taking me by the shoulders. I was still so limp that my head bobbled around.

I opened one eye a slit to look at her.

"You feel shitty now, but time will pass. Fletch and I will take care of you, and you'll heal. Really heal. Because you won't have to wonder if there's anything more you could have done. You made the big play. It didn't get the result you wanted, but the important thing is you made it. And, once you're better, you can make the big play with someone else."

"Yeah!" said Fletch.

"But here's something I know for a fact. If you don't get down there to be in these full cast photos, you'll regret it. Your production has had a dream run. You might not feel like celebrating, but Fletch is going to want to put the photos from tonight up on the wall at home, and they're going to feel sad if you're not in them."

I opened my other eye and looked at Fletch.

"What? Oh yeah, very sad. So sad," they said.

"But my make-up is all ruined," I said in a tiny voice.

Viv jumped up and clapped her hands together. "Oh, I got you girl. You don't play Fantine three shows a day back-to-back without learning how to turn tears back to smiles quick-smart. I've got wipes for running mascara, eye drops for redness, haemorrhoid cream for under-eye puffiness, saline for a blocked nose, and a full kit of super-strength waterproof make-up for touch ups."

My frown deepened. "You just have that stuff with you all the time?"

She ignored me. "And now we're going to fix you up, and you're going to fake smile in the back row of these photos like Idina Menzel after *Wicked* lost out at the Tonys to *Avenue Q.*"

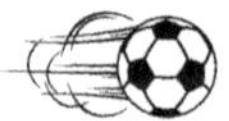

The party was a blur of shapes, camera flashes and noise. At one stage Ava and Allie had their arms around my shoulders as the team yelled the patriotic folk song *Waltzing Matilda.* I grimaced through it.

Someone shoved the big trophy into my hands and a bank of camera flashes blinded me.

Then I had some clear air around me. I took a deep breath in. The lights went down and loud dance music started up. The official team celebration portion of the evening was finished, and I was free to skulk back up to my room and bury myself in bedclothes.

I didn't want to look over toward the Americans. I couldn't deal with seeing Christine—stunning, smiling, relieved she'd dealt with me so she could move onwards and upwards.

But, as if coerced, I turned in their direction.

Across the room Christine stood alone, her back against the end of the bar. She wasn't smiling. I had learned to read her years ago, but right then her face was a complete blank.

My breath caught in my throat. I had dammed up all the hurt caused by her rejection, but the pressure of seeing her was causing the wall to crack. I felt hot anger at myself because in her green dress, to me she was still the most beautiful woman I had ever seen.

Her eyes met mine. She crossed her arms across her middle and her face remained frozen and blank.

Someone's hands were on my shoulders. "Come on, mate. Let's get you out of here," said Fletch.

They began to steer me away, but my feet were rooted to the spot.

Until Christine lowered her head and turned away.

She's done with me.

The dam wall broke. Fletch pulled me into a hug and I sobbed into their neck. They rubbed my heaving back and murmured, "There now, there, there, now," until I pulled it together enough to be led out of the party.

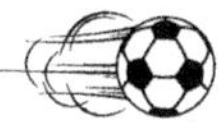

The following two days were truly one of those 'best of time, worst of times' situations you read about. They kept us in Sydney for media event after media event. Everyone else on my team was wildly happy twenty-four hours per day. I should have been too. But when I tried to conjure up joy over our victory I couldn't do it, although there were a few times when the realisation that I'd achieved great things with some of my best friends in the world made me glow a little on the inside.

Going back to that hotel room at the end of each day, the room where I'd begged Christine to stay and she'd turned on her heel and left me, was like a nightmare. In the hours spent there I yo-yoed between cringey shame that I'd been fooled by the same woman the same way twice, and anger, and sadness.

Viv had stayed in Sydney to look after me and listen to me wallow and cry. She was the only thing keeping me from bumming out Fletch and the rest of the team during the best week of their lives, so I was grateful.

On the third morning we were on the bus, finally on our way to the last tournament event. We pulled up to Bondi Beach. There was a crowd of thousands of people gathered on the grassy hill above the sand. Football Australia had wanted to give the general public a chance to see us hoist the Cup.

I looked out the bus window and sighed.

"Buck up, Mac," said Fletch. "Just a couple more hours and we can go home to Melbs and relax."

"Yeah, relax. And wallow. And pile every blanket in the house on top of me and never come out of bed."

They gripped my shoulder. "And heal."

I pressed my lips together in a thin smile.

"Just look out there. Can't get much better, hey?"

Our bus was parked on the road above the grassy hill that led down to the beach. Bathed in winter sunshine, the sea sparkled, and the golden sand shone. It was like Bondi was mocking my misery.

"I'm starting to hate this fucking city," I said under my breath as we got off the bus.

I trailed after my teammates onto the grass. A rope separated our path from the cheering crowd. Kids and adults alike called out to us.

"Allie, can I get a selfie?"

"I love you, Fletch!"

Then I heard a voice louder than the rest, calling my name over and over. It sounded like…

I stopped dead and swung around. Nope. Just a gaggle of kids hanging over the rope with posters and Sharpies. My stomach dropped like a rock.

"Keeley!"

The kids started shifting around as someone pushed in among them.

Christine.

"What…?" Shock ran through me, freezing me to the spot.

"Keeley! Oh, thank God. I thought I wouldn't make it in time. I need to talk to you."

Anger flared then fizzled, leaving me feeling tired. Bone tired of this rollercoaster I'd been on for four years. Tired of Christine needing me when it suited her, then leaving me behind.

"Now is not a good time," I said.

Her mouth snapped shut. She glanced around. The crowd directly around us had fallen silent, although I heard her name whispered by a few people. There were dozens of phones trained on her. The kids on her left and right stared up at her with their mouths open.

Her shoulders tensed as she took a deep breath. The silence stretched out.

Well, that's that. I went to turn and follow my team.

"Hold on! I'm sick of waiting for the right time," she said. Her voice was loud in the little pocket of hush that had formed around us. "I phoned my management. An hour ago. I've asked to play a season for Melbourne City starting December. Not your team, but the same city, so you can see as much or as little of me as you want. It's up to you.

"I've been an idiot. I thought being as disciplined as I needed to be to succeed meant depriving myself of what I wanted. I distrusted happiness, like it would make me lose my edge. Then, when the team lost, I told myself it was because I had let myself get distracted.

"I'm so sorry I hurt you, Keeley. I've been miserable. Looking back, the short times we've spent together have been the happiest of my whole life." Her voice cracked and became thick with tears. "You light me up. You're the best person I know. Please, please will you give me a second chance?"

All around her the mobile phones swivelled until they were trained on me. The heavy sadness I'd been carrying crumbled and fell away. I felt a golden lightness as my feet carried me forward.

I put my arms around her and kissed her. She tasted of salt, and I realised I was crying too.

The crowd had gone from silence to deafening cheers in an instant.

Someone slapped me square in the back.

"Ow!"

"Took you bloody long enough, Delacourt," said Fletch.

"I know, I know. I'll make it up to you, I promise."

"It's not me you need to make it up to," they replied.

Christine nodded. "I know. I will."

Fletch held her gaze for a couple of seconds then nodded and clapped me on the back again.

I caught sight of Coach, looking like a stunned mullet. She moved her mouth wordlessly, then said, "when I assigned you those hours of tape as homework and said, 'get to know her', this isn't exactly what I had in mind."

I laughed. Christine still had her arms around me and she gave me a squeeze.

Ava ran up. "Coach, Coach, I made out with the Danish goalie at the after-party the other night. Do I have your blessing to ask her out?"

Coach threw her arms into the air. "The tournament is over. We won. You all do what you want with your love lives, just leave me out of it!"

"Ava, can this team have one millisecond that doesn't revolve around you?" said Allie.

I wiped my face inelegantly on my sleeve and grinned at Christine. "You know this is your third chance. You totally blew your second."

Her lips curled. "True. But I'm the best striker in the world, and I'm not going to miss this shot. I promise."

Chapter 23

"Won't we hear room service when they knock?" I asked yawning.

"We might hear them, but I don't think I need hotel staff seeing me buck nekked first thing in the morning," Christine said.

I groaned and rolled over. "There's probably photos of us pashing at Bondi yesterday all over the internet. But now suddenly you're shy?"

She rolled away from me and stood up. "Come on. Let's get dressed and eat." She ripped all the bedclothes off me, including the sheet.

"Help! It's midwinter! I'll freeze," I said, still not moving.

"You're ridiculous," she said, walking back over to me. The sunlight on her skin in the morning light made my insides radiate pure warm joy.

She lay down full length next to me, clasping me tight in her arms. I kissed her slowly and fully. Desire sparked even though we hadn't slept much the night before.

"You can undress me again straight after breakfast," she said.

"I do love doing that," I said. "I might ask them to list it as a hobby on my Wikipedia page."

She scoffed. "Isn't 'undressing women' already listed on there as your occupation? As well as dumpster diving?"

"Oh, I didn't know I'd ordered a plate of 'being insulted' from room service just now. I thought I'd gone for the ridiculously overpriced eggs benny and a very big coffee."

"Hey, um, I didn't tell you the whole story yesterday."

"Oh yeah?" The worry-centre of my brain felt like it *wanted* to tingle but, holding this woman naked in my arms, it was impossible to feel anything but happy.

"Before I phoned management I phoned my sister. I told her what you said and then asked if I was making a big mistake by leaving you."

I smiled. "And what did Lori say?"

"She said I was being a stupid dumb idiot and I should be locked up in moron prison for even thinking of making a decision so foolish. She said that night—remember we got Chinese food when she came to visit?—I was different. Happier. Not thinking about the next training session or the next game, but having fun. Investing in someone other than myself."

"Shit, do Lori and Viv have bi-monthly debrief sessions or something? That sounds just like my little mate. She said I'd been skating over the surface of life ever since, you know…"

"I dumped you a week before Christmas?"

"Yeah, since then."

She propped herself up and pressed her forehead against mine. "I am so, so sorry," she said, then kissed my lips gently. "For everything."

"It's all right," I replied.

A few minutes later we opened the bedroom door and walked out into the living room of the hotel suite, Christine sporting one of my green-and-gold Matildas T-shirts.

"No photos, please. There'd be a few hardcore fans back home that already want to kick me out of the US for fraternising with the enemy," she said.

"Oh, hi," said Viv from across the living room.

She was wearing the exact same shirt as Christine.

"Viv, me old buddy! What are you doing here?" I asked.

"Oh, hi," said Fletch walking out of their bedroom and stopping short when they saw us.

"Hey, mate. Look, Viv's here."

"Uh, yeeeeah…" they replied.

"You're out and about early, Viv. Did you come over to have breakfast with us?" I asked.

Christine elbowed my arm.

"What, Chrissie?"

She raised an eyebrow and nodded toward Viv, then Fletch. Fletch looking sheepish and rumpled in a hotel robe, and Viv in her bright patriotic T-shirt. Fletch's T-shirt.

My jaw dropped. "Ohhhhhhhhh!"

"There it is," said Christine.

Fletch went to Viv and took her hand. "You don't mind, do you mate? I'm messing up the housemate dynamics a fair bit. But," they looked at Viv and smiled, "I've liked Viv for ages. But, you're my best mate and she's your best mate too and, I dunno, I was just scared. Then recently I started to think that you two were together and keeping it a secret from me."

I made a face and shook my head.

"There's no need to act quite so disgusted," said Viv.

"No! It's not that, it's just, we're like sisters, closer than sisters!"

"I know, I'm kidding," said Viv.

"Anyway, I know now you were acting super shady the whole tournament because you were sneaking around with Christine," said Fletch.

"Ohhhhh! Right," I said.

"But then," Fletch continued. "I saw how you and Christine just took a big old leap and went for it. You were so brave, Keels. And it didn't work out great at first because of you, Christine. Sorry. But then it was really good, you know?"

"I know," Christine and I said in unison. I put my arm around her and kissed her cheek.

"I decided I had to tell Viv how I felt. The truth will set you free, and all that. And it did."

"And I had thought they were hot from the first moment I met them. But as far as I knew they didn't see me as more than a friend. I mean, they were sweet and considerate and caring, but they're like that with absolutely everyone," said Viv.

"Aw, *you* are you mean," Fletch said, and leaned down and kissed her.

Watching them made my brain melt with cuteness.

I ran over to them. "Come 'ere, you massive, squishy marshmallows." I wrapped them both in a big hug. "My two bestest friends in the whole world. Hey, will you move into Fletch's room or vice-versa? If we get another roomie in maybe we can afford a PlayStation." I swung my head around. "Get amongst it, Chrissie!"

"Yeah, bring it in!" said Viv, disentangling one arm to extend it to Christine.

She walked over. "Oh, we're doing this? Uh, okay. Wow, that's tight. Y'all do this group hug thing a lot?"

"Every day before we leave the house," I murmured happily, pressing my cheek to Fletch's then hers.

I encircled my arms around them all tighter, like I wanted to keep this glorious happiness shining forever.

Epilogue

Ten months later

ADELAIDE UNITED BEAT BOTH MY Melbourne Victory and Christine's Melbourne City teams to take out the A-League Women's premiership.

A few weeks earlier I'd inked a contract to play for Seattle's team Reign in the US National Women's Soccer League for the next season.

Christine and I were flying to the States together in a few weeks, but Reign had sent over a jersey with my name on the back in advance. They wanted to get a jump on promos for the new season so had hired out a trendy Melbourne inner-city studio and asked Christine and me to pose for some photos.

"Did you have to travel far to get here?" the photographer in the bright white space had asked us when we arrived.

"Not really. We took the train from Footscray. Twenty minutes door-to-door," Christine replied.

When she'd arrived in Melbourne, she moved into a brand new flat in a Docklands highrise that her team had found for her. It didn't last long though. She'd officially moved in with me (and Viv and Fletch) by Christmas.

The four of us worked well as a household. Christine had even grown to enjoy our 'family breakfasts' of tofu scramble or almond milk millet porridge.

Viv and Fletch were loved up to the max. Fletch had scored a lucrative contract with a team in Iceland. Luckily their season was short up there, so they would be back in a few months. Long-distance was going to be a struggle, but they both knew when they'd be back together in person (the date was triple-circled with red love hearts on our kitchen calendar), and I had no doubt it would make them even stronger.

Viv's career was on an upswing too. She was about to set out on tour with the Australian production of *Mean Girls* the musical. She was in the chorus but also understudy to one of the lead roles, Gretchen Wieners, with the promise of being able to play the part in at least two Sydney matinees.

I was sad at the thought of our little house standing empty for so many months, but all four of us were going to land back there in November for the start of A-League pre-season and the long Melbourne leg of Viv's tour.

Christine and I changed into full navy and royal blue kit as instructed, and the photographer ushered us both in front of the bright hot lights.

"Oh, uh, the both of us?" I asked.

"Yes, um, I have the brief from Reign's marketing team here." She flipped through some stapled pieces of paper and handed them to us.

"Hah!"

"Oh my goodness, you're sure this is what they want?" Christine asked.

On the page was a line drawing of me and Christine smiling, with the words 'together at last' in big letters above our heads.

"Oh yeah," the photographer said, adjusting her chunky, black-rimmed glasses. "That's going to be a billboard at Pike Place market and on the Pacific Highway into town from Tacoma."

"Holy shit," I said. "I was going to check with them when we arrived if they wanted us to play our relationship down."

"But I guess not," said Christine.

"Most definitely not. They think your couple profile will boost interest and bring in record membership numbers. Now, are you ready to get your picture taken? Let's start with this one here," said the photographer, tapping the page with a purple fingernail.

I looked at Christine and shrugged, mouthing, "Couple profile?" with my back to the photographer.

She smiled back. "Let's do it."

We stood back-to-back with our arms crossed, smiling at the camera.

"I feel like we're in a '90s sitcom," I said.

"Or we're a moderately successful husband and wife real estate team with our ad on a bus stop bench," said Christine.

"Did you want to try something a bit more natural?" the photographer asked.

We took a few holding hands, then with her arm around my shoulder.

"That's great, that's great. I'm sure we've got plenty their marketing team can use. Thanks so much!"

"Thank you," we both said in unison.

Christine chuckled. "We have to stop saying the same thing at the same time, and—"

"Finishing each other's sentences," I said.

"And decrease our couple profile? No way, in fact, let's really give them something to slap on their billboards."

She leaned in and kissed me. I took her waist in my hands and pulled her close, slipping her more tongue than Reign could probably run as an Instagram tile without being sanctioned.

The camera flashed.

Other Books from Ylva Publishing

www.ylva-publishing.com

Perks of Office

Liz Rain

ISBN: 978-3-96324-661-6
Length: 178 pages (61,000 words)

Hapless office worker Emma is smacked with an instant crush on Bridget O'Keefe. Her new, untouchable, straight boss.

After a political scandal breaks, Bridget turns to Emma for comfort. Is it just a meaningless fling? Because there's no way ambitious, beautiful Bridget wants anything more from Emma. Is there?

A light-hearted, age-gap lesbian office romance.

Defensive Mindset

Wendy Temple

ISBN: 978-3-95533-837-4
Length: 376 pages (100,000 words)

Star footballer and successful businesswoman Jessie Grainger has her life set, and doesn't need anything getting in the way. That includes rebellious rival player Fran Docherty, a burnt-out barmaid with a past as messed up as her attitude. So when the clashing pair find themselves on the same Edinburgh women's football team, how will they survive each other, let alone play to win?

For the Long Run

Cheyenne Blue

ISBN: 978-3-96324-728-6
Length: 289 pages (90,000 words)

Runner Shan is tripped by a "koala", blowing her knee, and ruining her national team dreams. Life post-surgery will be hell as she lives on the fourth floor. Lizzie, the dream-wrecking koala, offers Shan her spare room. Their clashing lives and Shan's aloof training partner aren't ideal but they'll figure it out. Right?

An enemies-to-lovers lesbian sports romance about making it to the finish line.

The Long Shot

A.L. Brooks

ISBN: 978-3-96324-247-2
Length: 266 pages (93,000 words)

Talented golfer Morgan has never won a major but she's so close—no thanks to her famous, sexist, golfing dad.

Career-focused TV producer Adrienne is making a documentary on rising-star Morgan. The only problem is that the irritatingly attractive golfer treats Adrienne's plan like an invasion of privacy.

A lesbian sport romance on fierce desires and risking careers to win the ultimate prize.

About Liz Rain

Liz is from sunny Queensland, Australia and grew up doing lots of swimming, cricket and netball. She started a degree in journalism but decided early on she didn't want to be a journalist because she heard the hours were long and the pay was bad. She couldn't think of anything else she wanted to study, however, so decided to get the degree anyway.

After that she taught English in Japan, where she joined a soccer team to meet girls. Luckily the captain was a very nice American who is now her wife.

They live quietly in Logan, Queensland, with their two daughters, plus a dog named Pancake and a cat named Carly-Rae. Liz's interests are women's Australian Rules football (especially the Brisbane Lions) and teaching herself the mandolin off YouTube.

CONNECT WITH LIZ

Facebook: www.facebook.com/lizrainwrites

E-Mail: lizrainwrites@gmail.com

Onside Play

ISBN: 978-3-96324-824-5

Available in e-book and paperback formats.

Published by Ylva Publishing, legal entity of Ylva Verlag, e.Kfr.

Ylva Verlag, e.Kfr.
Owner: Astrid Ohletz
Am Kirschgarten 2
65830 Kriftel
Germany

www.ylva-publishing.com

First edition: 2023

Credits
Edited by Miranda Miller and Sheena Billet
Cover Design and Print Layout by Streetlight Graphics

Printed in Great Britain
by Amazon

25647628R00118